HOPES & DREAMS IN

Whitcomb Springs

A Collection of Short Fiction

From Award-Winning Author

MK McCLINTOCK

High in a mountain valley, a place for those who have
loved and lost becomes a home for those who wish to
hope and dream.

Trappers Peak Publishing
Montana
www.mkmcclintock.com

Hopes and Dreams in Whitcomb Springs; short fiction collection
ISBN: 978-1737758891

Cover Design by MK McClintock

AN ABRIDGED HISTORY OF
WHITCOMB SPRINGS

FOUNDED IN 1860 by Daniel and Evelyn Whitcomb, in what was then the Nebraska Territory, the mountain town of Whitcomb Springs started with a trading post (now the general store) and two cabins. Daniel and two friends from Pennsylvania, James Bair and Charles Carroll, founded the Whitcomb Timber Company in 1860. James Bair died the first winter after arriving in Montana, caught in a blizzard unawares. When the Civil War broke out in 1861, Daniel and Charles returned east to fight for the Union, believing it their duty to their country and their home state of Pennsylvania.

Evelyn had a choice to make—return home or wait for her husband, as Daniel promised to return soon. "The war would not last more than a few months," he had said. And so she chose to remain in Whitcomb Springs. Months became years, and under Evelyn's close watch and the help of a friend, the town grew year by year. The Whitcomb Timber Company added "Mining" to its name, and it continued to prosper. Nebraska Territory became the Montana Territory on May 26, 1864.

As families, tradesmen, and miners came to the mountain valley, Evelyn Whitcomb offered ownership in businesses to hard workers, benefiting both the town and its citizens, a number that reached one hundred and fifty souls by the end of the war.

Although the war did not extend to the Northwest Territories, the citizens of Whitcomb Springs feared for friends and family caught in the tumult. When the war ended in 1865, many who had built a life in the valley had lost and loved, prospered and hoped.

These are their stories.

PRAISE FOR THE SERIES

"What a wonderful story of courage and hope. I loved Evelyn Whitcomb's story and her love for her town and the families in it. How courageous she was. I hope we hear more about Evelyn and Daniel in future stories. I look forward to more short stories from this post-Civil War town."
~*Reader* on "Whitcomb Springs"

"Forsaken Trail is another fabulous read by MK McClintock! I have read just about everything MK has written and I am never disappointed. This one is no different. It is a short story but it is packed full of adventure, suspense, love and inspiration. I loved it! I give Forsaken Trail 5 stars and highly recommend Cooper's story for all who love a good historical."
~ *Reader* on "Forsaken Trail"

"Daniel and Evelyn Whitcomb had dreams together. However, when he returns home from the Civil War, he is not the same man. Along with their friends Cooper and Abigail, they will embark on a journey of hope and courage." ~ *Reader* on "Unchained Courage"

MONTANA GALLAGHER SERIES

Gallagher's Pride
Gallagher's Hope
Gallagher's Choice
An Angel Called Gallagher
Journey to Hawk's Peak
Wild Montana Winds
The Healer of Briarwood
Christmas in Briarwood

BRITISH AGENT NOVELS

Alaina Claiborne
Blackwood Crossing
Clayton's Honor
The Ghost of Greyson Hall

MCKENZIE SISTERS SERIES

The Case of the Copper King

CROOKED CREEK SERIES

The Women of Crooked Creek
Christmas in Crooked Creek

WHITCOMB SPRINGS SERIES

"Whitcomb Springs"
"Forsaken Trail"
"Unchained Courage"
"Whisper Ridge"

STAND-ALONE COLLECTION

A Home for Christmas

To learn more about MK McClintock and her books,
please visit www.mkmcclintock.com.

Dedicated to every hero you know.
Honor them.

WHITCOMB SPRINGS

In the spring of 1865, a letter arrives in Whitcomb Springs for Evelyn Whitcomb. The Civil War has ended and the whereabouts of her husband is unknown, but she doesn't give up hope. With courage, the help of a friend, and the love of a people, Evelyn finds a way to face—and endure—the unexpected.

"Whitcomb Springs" is the introductory, stand-alone story of the Whitcomb Springs series set in post-Civil War Montana.

WHITCOMB SPRINGS

Whitcomb Springs, Montana Territory
April 25, 1865

THE LETTER FLUTTERED to the table. Evelyn stared at the sheet of paper but could no longer make out the words as they blurred together. *Surrender.* She prayed this day would come, they all had, and after four tortuous years, the war was finally over.

There would be more capitulation on the part of the South, and too many families who would never see their men again . . . but it was over.

Separated, yet not untouched, from conflict, Evelyn Whitcomb lived in the same town her husband and their two friends founded one year before news of the Civil War reached them. By way of her sister, who lived in Rose Valley, Pennsylvania with their parents, they were kept informed as often as Abigail could get a letter through. Evelyn often wondered if she should have returned to Rose Valley to help with the war effort, much as her sister Abigail had done, yet she found the needs of Whitcomb Springs to be vast as the town continued to grow.

Many men and boys left, leaving their wives, mothers, and

1

sisters behind to fight for a cause they didn't fully understand, yet still felt it their duty to serve. Others remained behind to continue working in the mine and watch over those families with or without kin.

Evelyn read over Abigail's letter once more, letting the words settle into her mind, for even now she struggled to believe it was over—that her husband might return home.

> Dearest Evelyn,
>
> For too many years now I have shared with you the horrors and travesties befallen many of the young men with whom we spent our childhood. News has reached us that on the ninth of April, Robert E. Lee surrendered to Ulysses S. Grant at Appomattox Courthouse. Oh, sister, I dared not believe it was true when Papa brought home the news. He tells us not to become overly excited for there will surely be a few more battles waged until the news reaches both sides, but we can thank God that this war is officially over.
>
> Your news of Daniel's disappearance has weighed heavy on my mind these past months since we heard, and Papa has attempted to learn of his whereabouts, to no avail. We have not given up! There is much confusion right now on both sides and Papa said it could be weeks or months more before the men return home. Do not lose faith, sweet Evie.
>
> Your most loving sister,

Abigail

Evelyn pressed her face against her open handkerchief and wept against the cloth. The letter lay open on the table where it landed, for the moment forgotten. She did not have to witness smoke rising from destructed battlefields or watch neighbors' homes burn to ash like they did in the battle-worn regions back east, but Whitcomb Springs had not been spared from the emotional onslaught. Three husbands and two young sons had been sent home to be buried, including Charles Carroll, one of their partners in the founding of the town and mine. She wrote to Daniel when news of Charles's death reached his widow and young daughter, but Daniel did not respond for months, and even then it did not sound as though her letter about Charles's death found him.

He spoke of his love for her and of life after the war. They'd moved away from Pennsylvania five years prior, but he and Charles had still considered it their duty to fight. Friends since childhood, they did everything together, and going to war was no exception.

Evelyn slammed her fist on the letter and freed four years' worth of accumulated anger into her tears. As the town matriarch, even at her young age, Evelyn taught geography and history at the school, worked alongside the townspeople to establish a community garden, and offered whatever comfort she could to the wives and children whose men were lost or still away. She filled four years of days with enough activity to keep her too busy to feel the weight of the lonely nights. Alone now in the quiet of her parlor with her sister's letter dotted in tears, Evelyn relinquished herself to grief and the flood of memories from a happier time.

Nebraska Territory
June 15, 1860

"I WANTED ADVENTURE, Daniel, but I do believe you've gone too far this time." Evelyn dabbed her handkerchief against her neck. The air, still cool on the early summer day, warmed by degrees the farther they rode. It was her first time riding a horse outside a manicured park or gently sloping pasture, and the rough terrain proved to be more difficult than she'd originally credited.

Their guide, who went only by the name of Cooper, promised them what they'd see at the end of the trail would be worth the two days' ride to get there. Evelyn had seen beautiful scenery, but nothing so far as to make her trust the man whose appearance was as untamed as the trail on which they now traveled.

"We're almost there, Evie," Daniel said. He urged his horse forward so he rode beside his wife. "Didn't I tell you the West was spectacular?"

"Yes, you did." They were blessed with so much and yet they'd lost what was most important to them. Two children— sons—passed away shortly after their births, one year apart. They suffered together, mourned together, and dreamed together of a life far removed from their sorrows. He promised her adventure in a place grander than anything she'd ever seen. His promises were based on stories and reports of western expansion, and she loved him enough to believe in his dream as much as he did.

After weeks of train travel, cramped stage coaches, and a few

4

months' extended stay in Helena, Evelyn had endured enough dreaming. "Daniel, please tell our guide we must stop and rest."

Daniel pulled his horse to a stop, called out to Cooper, and helped Evelyn down from the saddle. The muscles in her back and legs were of little help to hold her upright. Daniel kept her steady, and she leaned toward him. He stood half a foot taller than her five and a half feet. Never one to be considered strong, he was lean and in excellent health from years of horse riding and exploring the Pennsylvania hills. When he asked if she wanted to remain in Helena while he joined the scout, she'd been quick to assure him she could handle the journey.

Four days of stage, wagon, and horseback, and she'd kept her silence until now. As though sensing she didn't want to get back on the horse, Daniel positioned an arm at her waist and told their scout they were going for a walk.

Cooper lifted the saddle off his horse and moved to do the same on the others. "Be sure you stick to the trail and don't go so far I can't hear you shout."

Evelyn glanced back at Cooper, wondering what event would require them to shout, and thought better of asking. She walked alongside her husband, staying on the trail as told. A steady rushing creek followed the trail as it widened, then narrowed. When they turned a bend around a copse of pine trees thick with branches and lush green needles, Evelyn stopped.

"Daniel." Her voice was a reverent whisper. She dropped his hand and stepped forward, her eyes moving back and forth over the landscape so as not to miss anything.

"I promised you, Evie." Daniel stood behind her and wrapped his arms around her waist. They were home.

Whitcomb Springs, Montana Territory
April 25, 1865

THE PIONEER MOUNTAINS, still capped with snow, rose above the hills surrounding their valley and the town. Breathtaking had been the first word uttered from her lips when she and Daniel stood at the edge of the valley. Evelyn picked up where her husband left off, and together they succeeded in building the town Daniel dreamt of, a town that would prosper without destroying the land.

The road was made passable their first summer, with a lot of expense, time, and hard labor of strong men hired to help build the first cabins and a trading post. Daniel promised he would build her a grand house, and it was the last thing he finished before he left.

The trading post was now a general store. Homes and businesses lined the carefully mapped roads, and last year they finished the church. Evelyn wondered what Daniel would say about the town when he returned. Pleased and proud, she hoped.

A gentle yet insistent knock at her front door drew her slowly from her own worries. Though more than two weeks had passed since the surrender, some would have heard the news and shared it with others until the whole town new. They did not have a telegraph or a post office yet, and letters from the East did not always reach them quickly. Townsfolk had families in the North and others in the South, yet here in Whitcomb Springs, they took no sides in the conflict of politics of war.

Evelyn blotted the tears away, took a few deep breaths, and rose from the chair. She wavered and kept herself upright by leaning on the table. Once her legs stopped trembling, she walked through the hall into the foyer. The knocking ceased, but a face pressed against the glass in the window, a cherub's face with red cheeks and wide brown eyes, surrounded by a halo of wispy blond hair.

The young girl waved and stepped back when Evelyn opened the door. "Missouri Woodward, you appear to have been in a spot of trouble." She looked over the girl's dusty dress, muddy boots, and a shawl covered in leaves.

Missouri grinned. "Monroe said girls couldn't climb trees because we're too puny."

"And you proved him wrong."

The six-year-old bobbed her head and straightened her shawl. "Mama won't be mad when I tell her. She says girls are just as cap . . ."

"Capable," Evelyn said while holding back a grin of her own.

"That's it. Mama says girls can do anything they want."

Evelyn believed Missouri's mother, a learned woman from Charleston and supporter of Elizabeth Cady Stanton, a leading figure of the women's rights movement, would teach her daughter to stand up for herself, but she also knew Lydia Woodward to be a lady of impeccable taste and manners. Evelyn held the door open and invited Missouri inside. "Your mother will understand, but even so, let's clean you up a little before you go home, and you can tell me what brought you to my door this morning."

Evelyn helped Missouri clean off her leather boots and remove the leaves and twigs from the shawl. She managed to wipe away some of the dust from the dress, but evidence of her shenanigans remained. From one of the few families in town of old money, Lydia Woodward had remained in Whitcomb Springs with her two children—Missouri and her older brother, Monroe—after her husband returned to Charleston to fight for the Southern cause. Lydia may have supported the beliefs of Elizabeth Stanton and feminist reformers, but she avoided the topic of reform when around Evelyn.

Women's rights were inevitable, this she believed, yet to speak of such things while her husband and so many other men and boys were at war somehow seemed disloyal to their sacrifices. From an established and wealthy family in Pennsylvania herself, Evelyn had everything she ever wanted, and her father encouraged an education beyond needlework and home management for his daughters. The stifling existence women like Lydia spoke of was foreign to Evelyn.

Even now, thousands of miles from home, she had both money and property. And she would give up both if only to have her husband back in her arms, to wake in the morning with him beside her, and to know he was safe—to know they would grow old together. She smoothed out Missouri's skirts and declared the girl fit enough to return home.

"Wait, Missouri. What brought you here, besides your dusty clothes?"

"Mama said Papa is coming home soon. Since you know everything and I guessed maybe if you said he was really coming home, it would be true."

Evelyn leaned back in the chair at the kitchen table and studied the girl. Hope, a useful commodity in the hands of the right person. Missouri Woodward possessed it in abundance. How to speak the truth without quashing hope? Evelyn wondered. If there was one way to quickly spread news of the surrender to those who had yet to hear, it was Missouri. "What has your mother told you about where your father has been these past years?"

"Protecting South Carolina. It's where I was born, and Mama said her mama and papa live there, but I don't get to see them anymore. I want to see them, but Mama said when Papa comes home we can go for a visit, so I really want Papa to come home."

It was not her place to explain the war to someone else's child, or to reveal the realities of life and death, so Evelyn chose her next words carefully. "Your father and many other fathers and brothers and sons are protecting their homes, but what caused them to fight is over now."

"Does that mean they're coming home?"

"Some of them will, and others won't."

The big brown eyes looked up at Evelyn. "You mean like when Mary's papa came back, and we all went to the cemetery?"

Evelyn lowered herself to the girl's level and squeezed Missouri's hands. "We don't know what comes next. However, we need to be strong for each other, no matter what. And you have so much hope in you; hold onto it."

Missouri nodded and fell against Evelyn. Her eyes remained dry, yet she held herself close for a few minutes before leaning back. "Sally Benson said my papa might not come home. Her mama is taking them back to . . ."

"Georgia."

"That's right."

Evelyn kept her sigh silent in the face of frustration. She'd heard of the Benson's decision to return to their native Georgia a few days ago. They were one of the families where husband and father had died, but there was no body left to send home.

"Missouri, I want you to promise me something."

"All right, Mrs. Whitcomb."

"No matter what you hear or what others say, remember to listen to your heart. Be strong and brave and never let anyone tell you your hopes are impossible."

"I don't understand, Mrs. Whitcomb."

Evelyn kissed the girl's cheek and said, "You will. Now run along to your mother. She'll wonder where you've gone."

With a quiet "thank you" and another quick hug, Missouri exited the house. Evelyn watched her run down the front walk and pass the beds of flowers eager to sprout and bloom before she remembered to slow down. One day soon, Evelyn thought, young girls will run and jump and play in the dirt without worrying if their fathers or brothers were coming back to them.

She stood on her wide front porch of the beautiful home Daniel had built, nestled in the untouched Montana valley. After four years of living without her husband, not knowing if he'd return to her, Evelyn still sought comfort from standing on the porch and looking up at the towering peaks. A few townspeople turned soil, preparing the community garden for seeds. Everyone who lived in town spent a few hours a week taking turns in the garden, and everyone reaped the benefits.

The community had been her family these long years, and she knew how blessed she was to want for nothing while others struggled. The garden had been a way to fill a need. She supplied the tools and seeds and looked forward to her turn to tend to the beds. The simple task of planting and watching the vegetables and flowers grow was a rewarding task.

She hired two of the young widows, Harriet Barker and Tabitha Armstrong, to help with her personal gardens and tend the house. Both women lived in rooms on the second floor, rooms that remained vacant and too quiet after Daniel left.

"Mrs. Whitcomb!" Lilian Cosgrove, who lived with her wounded husband in a small cottage on the other side of the meadow, hurried up the walkway. "Evelyn, please come quickly to the church."

Evelyn darted a glance down the road, but didn't see or hear a reason for Lilian to look flushed or to carry the heavy burden of worry in her eyes.

"Lilian, what's happened?"

Lilian darted a glance to the family across the way in the garden and lowered her voice. "There's something you need to see in the church. Ever since Reverend Mitchum left to tend that orphanage in San Francisco, Jedediah has been keeping a watch on the church, as you know. Today he found . . . oh, please come."

Bemused, though not surprised as Lilian had a tendency toward melodrama, Evelyn followed the woman down the street, past the small hotel, and into the meadow where the church stood. Daniel and Evelyn always meant for it to be a place of solace for anyone who stepped through its doors. It wasn't uncommon to find people passing through town, spending a few minutes inside before they moved on.

"Lilian, what is going on?" Evelyn stepped into the dimly lit building. The gray skies outside blocked much of the natural sunlight the row of windows often let into the church.

"You'll see, in the back."

Evelyn followed her friend to the back room where the reverend once lived. Sitting around the scarred table was a man, a woman, and a young boy, who looked no more than four years old, nestled on his mother's lap. Jedediah Cosgrove stood in front of the only exit.

The man at the table started to stand but quickly took his seat again. Evelyn moved her eyes to look at the man's legs. One appeared to be confined in a wooden leg brace. "Please, there's no need to stand." She took in the frightened expressions of the mother and child and looked at the others. "What's going on, Jedediah?"

"Jed saw her stealing from our garden," Lilian said. "He followed her here and found them living in these rooms."

Disappointment flooded through Evelyn's heart. She would speak with her friends later, but now, the couple and their children needed tending.

"There is no reason to be afraid. What are your names?"

The man again attempted to stand, but his wife pressed him down with a gentle touch and passed him their son. "Corbel. I'm Olive and my husband, Levi. This is our son, Elijah. We didn't mean any harm."

Evelyn was quick to reassure her. "I'm sure you didn't. I see you're injured, Mr. Corbel."

Olive spoke instead of Levi. "My husband doesn't speak, ma'am, not since . . ." she looked at her man, ". . . since he came home."

"I'm Evelyn Whitcomb." Evelyn turned to Lilian and Jed. "Thank you, Lilian, and Jed, it's okay. Please leave us. I'd like to speak with the Corbels."

"Are you sure it's safe?" Lilian asked.

Evelyn fought back the sadness at her friend's words. "Yes, I'm sure. I would like to visit with the Corbels alone for a few minutes. I'll come see you afterward." She rarely used her place in the community as a voice of authority, but when she did, those around her offered no argument. Evelyn waited until she heard the front doors of the church close.

When she faced the family again, Olive was still standing. "May I sit with you?"

Surprise replaced wariness and Olive nodded. Once Evelyn sat in the only empty chair, Olive followed suit. Evelyn said, "I'm sorry for my friends' behavior. They're protective when it comes to strangers."

"I shouldn't have stolen from them." Olive lifted her son back onto her lap. "We were traveling and sorry to say, we found ourselves off the trail."

"That's not difficult to do up here." Evelyn studied each of them, the gaunt faces and mended clothes. They were clean, indicating Olive's close care of her family. "Does the leg pain you, Mr. Corbel?"

He shook his head. "I can take it, ma'am." She barely caught his words. The hoarse whisper lost what little volume it had between them.

Evelyn cast a surprised look in Olive's direction. Olive explained, "I didn't tell you a falsehood, Mrs. Whitcomb. It's easier, you see, for people to think . . . Levi was scarred something fierce, and it pains him to speak."

"I am not accusing you of misleading me, not at all. How was he injured, if it's not too impertinent to ask?"

Olive and her husband exchanged a silent look, and he nodded once. Olive said, "He fought for the Confederacy. There was an explosion, but Levi prefers not to talk about it, ma'am. Not the explosion or the war."

"Please, call me Evelyn. And it's all right, I shouldn't have pried. Please accept my apologies. My husband hasn't returned home, and I don't know if he will, so I do understand a bit of what your family has suffered. Where are you going, if I may ask?"

"We're from Texas. When Levi was . . . after he returned, we lost our farm. We came north, heard there were opportunities up here, been finding work where we can." Olive sat higher in the chair, her back straightening as she held her son closer. "Are you going to turn us over to your sheriff?"

"As it happens, we don't have a sheriff right now."

"But we saw—"

"A sheriff's office, yes. We're a growing town and like to plan for the future."

"We saw a sign when we came into town: Whitcomb Springs. Is that you?"

Evelyn nodded. "My husband is Daniel Whitcomb. This town was our dream." Evelyn stood. "It's a place for new beginnings, if that's what you're after."

All three pairs of eyes met hers. Levi said in his whispered words, "Mrs. Whitcomb?" Those two words asked far more than a confirmation of her name. She couldn't help Daniel except with prayers, and right now she believed these people needed her attention more.

"These rooms are yours to use while you decide what to do next. There's a well out back and I'll have clean linens, food, and changes of clothes brought over. If you choose to leave, at least you will be rested. If you choose to stay, we will find a place for you and discuss your options."

"I don't understand, Mrs.—Evelyn."

"It's our way, Mrs. Corbel. There's work for those who are

willing to work hard and there's a home here for those in search of one. Life in Whitcomb Springs is not always easy. It's rewarding, and the community is strong, and most importantly, it's ours." Evelyn saw from the way they looked at her that she'd given them enough to think about. "I'll send someone along with the items I mentioned. If you'd like to visit again, my house is down the north road past the general store. I would like to help if you'll let me."

Evelyn left them to their privacy. She didn't know if she'd see them again or if in the night they planned to disappear in hopes of reaching a new destination. Either way, there was another matter to tend, one she dreaded.

Lilian and Jed weren't waiting outside. She walked to the edge of the meadow and crossed the bridge over a narrow point of Little Bear Creek. They stepped outside when she approached.

"Have then gone?" Lilian asked.

"They are welcome here, Lilian, as you and Jed were five years past."

"They stole from us."

Evelyn's heart ached at the other woman's harsh words. "True, and I suspect they will repay you in any way they can. Where is your charity, Lilian, and yours, Jed? You were injured and by grace you came home to your wife. Others have suffered far more. Olive had a son to feed and only a mother's desperation would have had her committing a crime, but it is a minor one. She stole food from your garden to feed her son, food that can be replaced. They are to be forgiven."

Jed stepped forward, chagrined. "I'm sorry, Mrs. Whitcomb. You're right. I don't reckon I know what would have become of Lilian and me if we hadn't found this town, or if I hadn't come back to her."

"I appreciate—"

"But I ain't never stolen."

"I see." And Evelyn did.

Lilian held a white cloth in one hand and her other still showed evidence of flour from baking. "This town isn't for people like them. We've worked too hard."

Evelyn fought back tears for the loss of two people she'd called friends—family, even. "I know well enough what kind of people belong in this town. People like the Corbels. These mountains that surround us, the valley where we build our homes and grow our crops, don't belong to us. We put our name on a sign and erected this town. We burrowed into the earth so the mine could support the town and the people in it, and when we're done, we do everything we can to make the land whole again. We don't take what we don't need, and we give what we can. That has always been Whitcomb Springs." Evelyn walked away, stopped after a few feet and looked back at them. "At what point did you forget?"

EVELYN WIPED THE back of her sleeve over her damp brow. The spring morning brought with it rare sunshine and a sky as blue as the wild flax sprouting in the meadows. An early rain softened the soil, allowing her cultivator to move effortlessly through the rich, brown earth. She relished the hour she spent every morning in her flower beds before she took a turn at the community garden.

Harriett cut a spade into the dirt a few beds away, leaving Evelyn to enjoy the quiet of her own thoughts. One of the kitchen windows was open to let in the cool air and out wafted the scent of Tabitha's culinary talents. There would be fresh baked bread and a sweet pastry of some sort to sell in the general store. Evelyn would see to it that the Corbels received a healthy ration of bread, baby vegetables from the garden, meat from Evelyn's personal stores, and of course something sweet for young Peter.

A maze of old roots latched onto the hand tool, and with expert skill, Evelyn searched the ground until her fingers touched a bulb. She brought it closer to the surface and recovered it before moving onto the next section. Evelyn much preferred gardening to kitchen work. She learned what was needed to so she and Daniel wouldn't starve during those early days in their new home. Tabitha lost her husband in a hunting accident soon after they moved to Whitcomb Springs, and though the circumstances came with sadness, Evelyn thanked the Lord every day for Tabitha.

Harriett's husband made her a widow six months after they married on her twentieth birthday. After a year under Evelyn's roof, the young woman had yet to share how her husband died. Whispers among the townspeople about what might have happened dispelled when Evelyn stood up and vouched for Harriett. These women were as much her sisters as the one she left behind in Pennsylvania.

She sat back on her heels and straightened the stiffness from her body. A twinge in her lower back told her she'd been working longer than planned. She removed one of her leather gloves, long ago ruined for anything except manual labor, and pulled Daniel's watch from her apron pocket. A gift from his father when they had left home to come west, Daniel had asked her to keep it close while he was gone, to remind her he would return. Evelyn kept it polished and with her, always. The face indicated nine o'clock, and she tucked the gold watch and chain back into her pocket.

She looked at the expansive community garden next to hers. It had started out as a way to serve her, Daniel, James, and Charles, but as others came to help build the town—and stay— Evelyn saw a new need arise. Many families had small gardens to feed their own, but many contributed to and enjoyed the bounty from the town's garden. The Wiley family would arrive in another hour for their turn.

They had a few weeks yet before most of the vegetables sprouted, and longer still until many of them were ready to harvest. In the meantime, most families, herself included, subsisted off canned vegetables and fruits. A small greenhouse, finished last summer, provided fresh vegetables throughout the year, rationed, of course.

Evelyn remembered the Shelton Estate Greenhouses her family once visited in Massachusetts. Impressive in their scale and variety of plants within, they sparked an idea in Evelyn that took root. She had received skepticism when she'd explained to Cooper what she wanted built on the land near her home. Close enough to access when the weather turned inclement, yet far enough away for the house not to block the sunlight. Wasted expense, Cooper had told her, and impossible to get someone to haul the supplies she needed. Evelyn ignored him and endured the murmurs from the townspeople, even as she paid dearly for materials and labor. When the structure was complete, raised beds built inside, and the first seeds planted, doubt turned to gratitude.

No one in town knew the extent of her family's wealth, not

even Cooper. She'd heard stories of the eccentric Whitcomb woman who decided to build a town on her own in the remote mountain valley of Montana. No one seemed to remember Daniel or that without him, she never would have ventured this far. Or would she have? Evelyn sometimes wondered if she longed for adventure because it's what she wanted or because Daniel's thirst for it was contagious. Either way, she'd found her place and people who needed her.

Harriett stepped between Evelyn and the morning sun, casting a shadow that made it possible for Evelyn to tilt her head back without squinting. Harriett, with a spade in hand and dirt on her apron, said, "Are you all right, Evelyn? You look as though you took to wandering in your mind for a spell."

Evelyn smiled, braced a hand on the fence, and pushed up to her feet, much like a toddler does when they're learning to stand. She'd been on the ground without respite for almost two hours. "I suppose I was." She shifted her eyes to look over the area where Harriett had been working. "The gardens get lovelier every year. The soil is rich, and we had a good winter. If the rain and sun continue to share the sky these next months, we can expect a good crop from the community garden."

"More food will be a blessing. Purdy Lutts got a letter yesterday from her kin in Missouri. Her son is gone now, too, and just a few months after her husband."

News, gossip, and sickness moved quickly through a town the size of Whitcomb Springs. The only people who wouldn't know about Purdy Lutts's recent loss lived on more isolated farms and small ranches outside town. Soon enough, they would all come into town to order or pick up supplies, and when they left again, it would be with full wagons and the latest happenings.

Harriett continued. "And Betty Miles had a letter from her husband, too. He's lost an arm and won't be able to work out here. He's sent for her. She doesn't want to live in Florida with his folks, but she's got no choice."

"Harriett, how do you always hear of these things before everyone else?"

"I make sure I'm working in the general store when the supply wagon comes through."

Daniel had negotiated with a driver in Butte to deliver supplies once a month to their fledgling homestead. It took buying the man a new wagon and a healthy pair of strong mules before he agreed. Most supplies took weeks or months to arrive as there was yet no train into Montana. The trips to Whitcomb Springs turned out to be a profitable venture for the driver since he stopped at two other small communities when making the trip. As the town slowly grew, once a month turned into twice. The mail came through on the same wagon, which meant most folks getting a letter received news on the same days as everyone else.

Exceptions were made, of course. The worst of news traveled faster, if whoever sending the news could afford a private courier, but that was rare. Evelyn had received a few such letters from her family, as did other families of means in the town, but most had to wait and worry.

Evelyn gathered her tools and dropped them in a basket along with the pulled weeds. "I am sorry to hear about Betty's eminent departure. I'll pay her a visit today, and one to Purdy as well."

"I don't know what Purdy will do with both her son and husband gone. She and that little girl don't have much."

Harriett had left home without an education beyond basic

reading and numbers. Evelyn and Daniel brought with them a small library of books, and Evelyn saw to it that Harriett read a little every day. She'd also tutored her in etiquette, but there were still times when the young woman's early lack of education showed through, ·as in this case, where she spoke abruptly without checking to see if others were about. Tabitha stood in the kitchen doorway behind Harriett. At least it had only been Tabitha and not someone else from town. They had an unspoken agreement in the house that whatever was said among them stayed there. News trickled down the dirt roads quickly enough without them helping it along.

Tabitha stepped on the grass and crossed to where they stood. "Purdy lost her son?"

Harriett looked up at Tabitha, who stood a few inches taller. "Oh." She glanced all around to find they were alone. "I shouldn't have said anything out here."

Evelyn brushed off her apron and picked up her basket. "No matter now. Word will reach everyone soon enough. Let's clean up and then I want to sample whatever heavenly treat Tabitha has whipped up in the kitchen."

The three women walked back into the house, but on the porch, Evelyn stopped and turned to look up at her mountains. Dark gray clouds hovered over a few peaks, and soon they would overtake the sun for control of the sky. A breeze picked up and forced the trees and low grass beyond the fence to sway. Evelyn sensed a shift in the air, and she wished she knew whether it was the atmosphere or an omen of dark things to come.

EVELYN SET HERSELF to the difficult task of consoling her

friend, except when she arrived at the small cabin a half mile east of town, Evelyn met with a surprise. Purdy's disposition was not that of a woman who only yesterday heard of her son's death. She smiled in greeting when Evelyn walked up carrying two baskets, one she would leave with Purdy and the other she'd take to the Corbels.

"Hello Evelyn!" Purdy unhooked the last dry sheet from the clothesline and lifted the basket of clean linens. "I hope you'll join me for an early tea. I have plenty to spare." Like a prairie wind, Purdy hurried indoors without a wasted step. She continued talking about the weather, the progress of the mine, and the new baby born last week. She mentioned nothing of the letter or her son.

She left Evelyn to follow her inside and motioned for her to have a seat while she put away the wash. Purdy moved through the motions of placing tea and fresh scones on the table. Evelyn didn't mention it was hours before teatime or that Purdy rarely baked since her husband and son went to war.

"Won't you sit and join me, Purdy?"

Purdy stopped and looked at Evelyn. Her eyes stared at Evelyn with a blank expression for several seconds before her hands started to shake. She shook her head and returned to kitchen work. "I can't stop. Not for a minute, for a second. I can't stop."

Evelyn rose from the chair and reached for Purdy. The other woman's body tightened when she stepped back a foot. She raised tear-filled eyes to Evelyn. "I can't stop. If I stop, it's real." Evelyn's arms went around Purdy's shaking body. Tears trickled down her cheeks and sobs tore from her lips. A few minutes into the uncontrolled release of grief, Evelyn saw the terrified face of a young girl peek around the corner into the kitchen. A few soft tears fell from the young girl's eyes before she moved out of sight.

An hour later, Evelyn walked away from the cabin. Tabitha had arrived and promised to watch over Purdy for the remainder of the day. No doubt others would stop into visit, either to offer condolences or hear the news firsthand about the latest young man who would not be returning to Whitcomb Springs.

Evelyn walked down the main road through the center of the small town. They'd made great progress in four years, from essential businesses to new homes. The hotel, an extravagance for their town, remained empty most of the time, but she held hope that one day the beauty of the mountains would attract visitors looking for a quiet respite and restorative holiday. Cooper still acted as a guide, bringing the occasional visitor or surveyor through. They often spent a few evenings in town before moving on. Last year a photographer came through to capture images so he could put them on display in St. Louis. Yes, she had dreams for Whitcomb Springs, but above all, she dreamed of keeping the town a safe place for those who lived and worked there.

A loud rumble brought her to a halt outside the general store. She noticed a few others also stopped what they were doing to investigate the noise. Another rumble, this time joined by a distant sound of thunder. They all looked up. Other than the dark clouds Evelyn saw earlier, the sky was clear.

Shouts not understood but far enough away to be heard repeated in a chain reaction that traveled from one person to the next until they reached her. A tree snapped. Ropes broke. Avalanche. Evelyn caught enough snippets to know a terrible accident had happened in the logging camp. She left the basket for the Corbels on the general store porch and hurried down the road. She stopped at the blacksmiths to borrow a horse from Dominik Andris.

He already had one saddled for himself. He quickly saddled a mare, helped Evelyn on the horse, and together they followed others who made their way north of town. Cooper caught up with them before they veered onto the timber trail. Three miles up the mountainside, on a narrow stretch of open land, the original logging camp sat empty. Evelyn urged her horse forward, but Cooper grabbed the reins and shook his head. "You go up there right now, they'll worry more about you than getting everyone out alive."

Since the day Cooper McCord led her and Daniel to the valley they now called home, he'd always been straight with her, even if she disliked what he had to say. Their relationship was unique; they were the truest of friends. Had she not been married . . . Evelyn didn't want to think about the possibility. She trusted Cooper, and when it came to life and death situations, she listened. "You're going up there?"

Cooper nodded. "Dominik and I will ride up and see what's happened. Don't go up there, Evelyn."

It was the first time he'd called her Evelyn in front of others. "I won't. Please be careful, both of you."

She dismounted and tethered her horse to one of the posts in front of the foreman's cabin, the closest structure to where she stood.

Half the number of men from the town remained at home rather than fight in a war they didn't understand at the time. Some refused to leave their families behind while others didn't believe in taking up arms. Evelyn had made the decision to keep both the timber operation and the mine going these four years for the sake of the town and the families who relied on steady wages. She visited once a month, much to the concern of Cooper who always accompanied her. He worried not about the men who lived in Whitcomb Springs but the few who hired on during busier seasons, men who were passing through looking for temporary work—men who couldn't be trusted.

The man they carried down on a makeshift stretcher was no stranger passing through. She recognized him as Tabitha's older brother, William Lee, who lived and worked at the logging camp six months of the year and spent the other six months in Wyoming. He came to Whitcomb Springs after Tabitha's husband had died, and though Evelyn knew him only in passing or for the occasional meal he took at the house, he was family.

They eased the stretcher to the ground, not far from the foreman's cabin. Cooper knelt next to the body and held a hand over William's mouth to check his breathing. When he looked up, he searched the crowed until he found her. Evelyn knew William was gone.

EVELYN FOUND TABITHA in the kitchen. She stood at the long and tall wooden table near the wood stove, her hands covered in flour as she turned dough in a bowl. Her soft humming filled the air with a sweet and hopeful melody. Evelyn didn't recognize the song. The windows near the stove were open to let in the cool, fresh air, though Evelyn still noticed a hint of perspiration at Tabitha's brow. Two pies cooled on a small table away from the heat and a delicious scent wafted from the vicinity of the stove. Her friend had been busy and Evelyn knew kitchen work was Tabitha's solace, her greatest joy. Evelyn had given some thought recently to opening a small cafe for Tabitha to run, but selfishness had kept the idea at bay for too long.

Would Tabitha remain in Whitcomb Springs, Evelyn wondered? She took another step into the kitchen and Tabitha looked up, her lips formed in a wide smile.

"Evelyn! You're back sooner than I expected." Tabitha glanced out the window. "Or I've been at this longer than I thought. A cake will be ready soon. It's a new recipe I thought could be used for our picnic on Sunday after church." Tabitha wiped her hands, covered the bowl of dough with a clean cloth, and brushed fallen strands of hair off her face. It was then her smile slowly faded. Her eyes widened, and she bit her lower lip. Evelyn had seen that expression on her friend only once before—when her husband died.

"Evelyn?"

She crossed the kitchen but Tabitha held up a hand to stop her from coming closer.

"I want to visit but I really need to clean up and get lunch ready for William. I promised him a special treat today." Tabitha pointed to the pies. "Apple is his favorite. I can extra apples every year so he always has pie in the early season." Her eyes filled with tears. "He's coming down the mountain so we can sit in the gardens. There aren't many blooms yet, but he loves the garden." Tabitha removed the cloth on the dough not yet risen and began to punch it down in the bowl.

"Tabitha." This time Evelyn placed her arm over the other woman's shoulder, a gentle touch that set Tabitha back.

"No." Tabitha shook her head and pushed the bowl away, stepped closer to one of the open windows. "You can't say the words, not yet."

Evelyn stood in silence while Tabitha's breathing became more erratic and tears slid down her cheek. The front door opened and Harriett hurried into the kitchen. She looked first at Tabitha and then to Evelyn. "Is it true what they're saying about William?"

Evelyn kept her silence, for no words were needed to confirm the truth. Another man of Whitcomb Springs had perished. This time, not from war, yet Evelyn knew Tabitha's loss would be as sharp and unyielding as when she'd lost her husband.

"I knew." Tabitha's breathing calmed, and she held a hand over her heart. "When I saw you, your face . . . it was like when James died. When you told Harriett her husband was gone. The same face. The noise earlier . . . I thought it was thunder, a storm coming. I imagined sitting on the porch with afternoon tea, watching the rain . . ." She turned toward the window and leaned against the wall. "William loved summer. He told me this year he was staying in Whitcomb Springs for good, not going back to Wyoming in the winter. He wanted to raise horses here." She turned tear-filled eyes to Evelyn and Harriett. "It wasn't his time."

It wasn't any of their times, Evelyn thought. Sensing Tabitha needed space but not solitude, she remained where she stood. Harriett must have sensed something else because she approached Tabitha, draping an around her friend's shoulder. It was then Evelyn understood. Harriett had lost a husband, Evelyn had not. Harriett knew—absolutely knew—of Tabitha's suffering. This time the sadness was for the loss of a sibling, but still a penetrating loss to which Evelyn could not relate.

The snap of a rope and a tree fallen in the wrong direction sent William to his death, without time even to say goodbye to his sister. Too many never got the chance to say goodbye. Would Evelyn be one of them?

She walked quietly from the room and past the door Harriett had left open in her haste. She stood on her front porch listening to the sounds of the small town and thought of Daniel.

THREE DAYS HAD PASSED since William's death. Harriett and Evelyn stood on either side of Tabitha in front of his grave. Rich, brown earth covered the wood coffin Cooper had built, and most of the town huddled in the cemetery near the church. Set back from the road, across the meadow and near a year-round stream, a dozen graves with bodies, and more without, dotted the well-tended ground. The first body they'd buried was of James Bair, one of Daniel's childhood friends and a founder in the Whitcomb Timber Company. He perished his first winter, caught in a blizzard, leaving no wife or children behind. Charles Carroll, the third founder in the timber company, died three years into the war. His body was sent home to Pennsylvania and his wife and daughter soon followed. Evelyn was tired of burying men. No woman or child in Whitcomb Springs had passed away in those four years. Perhaps God decided to show mercy on them, Evelyn thought, or perhaps their time would come.

For the first time in four years, Evelyn experienced true doubt for the future coupled with an anguish that gripped her heart, encasing it in despair. They waited together by William's grave long after the townspeople departed. Olive and Levi Corbel, with their son Elijah, waited near a large oak outside the fenced-in cemetery. Evelyn met Olive's gaze and motioned for them to come forward. As a unit, the young family walked across the grass and stopped a few feet from the fresh grave.

"We wanted to offer our condolences," Olive said, and held out a small bunch of wild buttercups. It wasn't an easy flower to find in their valley, which meant Olive had taken care and time to search for the spring wildflower. "I lost my young brother to fever three years ago. It's a loss that stays in you deep, right here." She tapped her chest above her heart. Elijah grasped his mother's hand when she stepped back, his eyes wide with curiosity at the exchange.

Levi tried to speak, his words barely discernible. "Anything we can do?"

"There's nothing." Tabitha stared at them, the flowers in one hand and the other gripped tightly in Harriett's palm. "Thank you for these. William would have liked them."

Evelyn left Harriett to look after Tabitha while she walked toward the church with the Corbels. She didn't venture too far in case her friends needed her. No, not just friends. They were her family. The townspeople, the strangers who passed through, they were her family, too. She said to the Corbels, "It was kind of you to bring the flowers."

"I heard about the young man who died, heard it was her brother."

Evelyn nodded. "News moves quickly here. His loss will be felt for a long time to come."

Olive hesitated with her next words, but with some encouragement from her husband, she said, "Did you mean what you said about us staying on?"

"I did. We'll find a place for you, if you want to stay."

"I can work. Levi can't talk well, or ride, but he has a good mind and knows about the land. We'd like to farm again, and . . . we can't think of anyplace we'd rather go, leastways not right now."

"It so happens we could use another good farmer in Whitcomb Springs."

ANOTHER WEEK DRIFTED by, and Evelyn waited. Three men returned home to their families. Two wives received word that their husbands died in final battles: one at Appomattox and another at the Battle of West Point, a day after President Lincoln's assassination. Another woman heard from her son who said he wasn't ready to return home. Life continued forward. Evelyn dug her spade through the damp earth. Two days of heavy rain had left plants and seedlings wilted, but the sun peeked around the edge of a thick pillow of clouds pushing away the gloom. Tabitha worked nonstop in the kitchen, volunteering to teach some of the children about cooking, digging in the community garden at least twice a day, and filling in at the general store whenever she could. Evelyn and Harriet worried but said nothing. Tabitha slept and ate, relieving some of their concern, but she kept her body and mind too busy to think of her brother.

"Evelyn?"

Evelyn shifted and smiled at Olive. "Welcome, Olive. How lovely to see you." She pushed herself up from where she knelt in the dirt and brushed away a few clumps of mud. "Do you have time for tea?"

"That's kind of you, but I need to be getting back. I came to deliver these letters that arrived with the supply wagon." Olive held out three envelopes, which Evelyn accepted.

"Thank you, Olive. One of us usually picks up the mail at the store. This is a treat." Evelyn marveled at the change in Olive in the short while since she started to work two shifts a week at the general store and two more at the hotel. Gone was the gauntness and burden of fear. No longer did she need to worry about her next meal or wonder where her family would lay their heads at night.

The Corbels worked hard and went beyond earning their keep. The two acres of land that once belonged to James Bair, along with the tidy cabin, suited the family's needs. They kindly declined further help, already overwhelmed at the kindness shown to them by most of the townspeople.

Evelyn noticed Olive looking over the established gardens. James Bair's plot of land had gone untended the past four years. Evelyn saw to it that the cabin was kept in good repair, but the land was left to nature's devices. "How is the clearing coming along?"

Olive faced her again and smiled. "A quarter acre is almost ready for planting. The Dockett boy, Timothy, has been a big help to Levi."

Evelyn heard of Timothy Dockett, a young man of sixteen years, helping the Corbels. She doubted they could pay much, even with the extra she paid Olive for her work at the general store. It was precious little extra, for the proud woman refused charity. She paid Jed and Lilian for the vegetables stolen in desperation, an action which had surprised Lilian and left Jed wondering if he'd been wrong about the newcomers. "I know

Timothy is grateful for the work. He has his heart set on attending college."

"Oh he's been wonderful for Levi to have around. It will be years yet before Elijah can help with farming, and by then—"

"By then, anything can happen," Evelyn finished for her. "Will you come for tea tomorrow? If you have time."

Obviously surprised at a second invitation, Olive nodded. "I'd like that. I did want to ask . . . how is Mrs. Armstrong fairing?"

Evelyn made sure neither Tabitha nor Harriett were in hearing distance. "She's better. It takes time."

Olive nodded, asked Evelyn to give Tabitha her good wishes, and she walked back down the road. Harriett approached and said, "Folks are taking well to the Corbels. I've visited a time or two. The young one, Elijah, is a good boy." There was a wistfulness in Harriett's voice. She'd lost a child at birth, shortly before her husband passed. That loss held pain to which Evelyn could relate.

"Harriett, would you do something for me?"

"Of course."

"I want to gather a few seedlings, both vegetables and flowers, for Olive. She mentioned they'll have enough land cleared soon to start planting."

"I don't reckon she'll accept them, unless she buys them."

"I'll figure something out."

EVELYN SAT AT the desk in her parlor and read over the first letter from home. One of the letter's Olive dropped off had been from Tabitha's family. Evelyn knew Tabitha's parents lived in Oregon and hoped one day their daughter would return. Tabitha confessed once that she and her mother didn't get along too well. She faced a difficult decision, and Evelyn worried for her.

The other two letters were from Pennsylvania: one from her mother and the other from her sister. As her sister didn't sweeten the truth, whether the news was good or bad, Evelyn read her mother's letter first. She wanted to put off any potential bad news a little longer. Her mother spoke of news from their acquaintances and a few social events to celebrate the end of the war. She mentioned two young men Evelyn knew in her youth, who had not returned. She moved quickly past the sad news and recounted details of new improvements to the house and gardens. It was her mother's way of coping, and Evelyn didn't begrudge her. The letter ended with a request for her to return home now that the war had ended.

She set her mother's letter aside and opened Abigail's.

Dearest Evelyn,

I shan't wait on the most important news, which I imagine you've waited for long enough. Daniel is alive!

Evelyn gasped and released a shaky breath. Her hands shook as she continued reading.

Papa doesn't know where he is, but reports do not list Daniel among any dead or in field hospitals. It will take time yet to find everyone who has gone missing. Even now Daniel could be on his way to you. Oh, Evie, I do hope he is! He has not sent word to his family, but I pray you do not take his silence as anything except a husband eager to get home to his wife. I pray to see you both again soon. I have missed you, dear sister.

My next news will no doubt shock you—I wish to visit you in Montana. Five years ago you left, and four of those burdened by war. It has been far too long, and I do hope you will not try to talk me out of coming. Will you consider Mother's request? She told me how much she longs to see you again, and I know Papa is of a similar mind. I explained to them both that surely you could not leave when Daniel must be on his way to you. Your letters these past years have painted your new home in such vivid wonder, and I long to see it for myself. I have not spoken to Mama or Papa of my plans. They will most certainly disapprove, yet I feel I must do this. I miss you, Evie.

Yes, it is decided. I was uncertain in my conviction to travel such a great distance. After all, you are the adventurer in the family, but now I am resolved in my plans. Please do not tell them. I promise I will speak with them soon, and I shall write to you of my arrival.

Be well and safe, Evie, and please do not fear. I feel in my soul that Daniel will return. Never have I known two people more destined to love for all time.

Your most devoted sister,
Abigail

TWO DAYS LATER and Evelyn still thought of her sister's letter. Abigail was the sensible and dutiful daughter, not prone to fanciful thoughts. And yet, she desired to leave home. Their parents would not allow their beloved young daughter to travel such a distance on her own, but who would they send with her? Abigail had been right about one thing—Evelyn had no plans to leave Montana, not when Daniel might still be alive.

She sat in the rocking chair on her front porch, enjoying the dance of clouds and sun over the mountain peaks. Snow still capped the highest of the mountains and the recent rains had brought a brilliant green to the valley. After an early morning in her gardens and her weekly visit to the general store, Evelyn considered new possibilities for the town. A few buildings remained empty, including the sheriff's office and medical clinic. The town wasn't large enough to warrant either on a regular basis, yet she felt strongly that both the position of sheriff and doctor should be filled.

She sat up and walked into the house. Her desk in the parlor faced the mountains and overlooked her gardens. The window stood open and Evelyn relished in the cool air and sweet fragrance of tall grass and freshly tilled soil. She picked up the handblown glass stylus her father had given her before she left home and dipped it into the ink well. She gathered her thoughts and set pen to paper, outlining the details of an advertisement for a doctor.

A few individuals in town knew enough to patch up injuries, but she wondered if a real doctor could have saved young William. Her inheritance was great, and the income from the timber and mining companies had only increased hers and Daniel's wealth. If she could not use the money to help the people entrusted in her care, what right did she have to it? Finding a doctor willing to live in a remote Montana valley might prove difficult, Evelyn thought.

She next penned an advertisement for a sheriff. Before she made copies and mailed them off to the nearest newspapers, and those as far off as St. Louis, she would approach Cooper about the position. Thus far he'd been willing to step in whenever the need for peacemaking arose, which wasn't often. Reluctant to accept a position that kept him in town, Cooper preferred to keep his freedom to roam and hunt when the mood suited him. Evelyn never mentioned to him that he rarely left town, always close by in case she needed him.

Their friendship deepened every year since Daniel had left. Evelyn once asked him why he did not go to fight, but he changed the subject without explanation. Despite what he wanted people to believe of him, she often wondered if there was more to Cooper than he allowed even her to see.

Thoughts of Cooper brought her mind back around to her husband. After three more weeks and too many nights crying herself to sleep, Evelyn began to lose faith that Daniel was alive. Abigail's contagious optimism had given Evelyn hope for a week, then two, but three? And still no word?

Harriett called out from the front garden. When Evelyn looked up, she moved her eyes to follow where Harriett pointed. She could not see the road and moved to the front door where she stepped outside.

"Harriett, what do you see?"

Harriett hurried around the side of the house and Tabitha stepped onto the porch beside Evelyn. Harriett said, "He's coming this way." She pointed and Evelyn's gaze followed. The sun shined into her eyes and she raised a hand to shield them. A lone man in dusty clothes with a beard grown too thick walked toward them. The road leading north of town led into the mountains. Those passing through traveled west or south to the mining camp looking for work.

Evelyn stepped out from beneath the protection of the covered porch, down one step then another. The man's gait was almost regal. He stood tall and straight, much taller than her. She peered closer trying to see his face. He stopped and a smile slowly formed on his face. He held open his arms, and Evelyn ran.

ALONE IN THEIR bedroom, the early morning light flitted across Daniel's face. She wept in his arms the night before, then loved him as she imagined doing for so long. His face was now clear of the thick beard and she gently touched a finger to the long puckered scar on his jaw. There'd been no words between them after he had bathed and ate. They relished in each other's presence, both realizing that soon enough the many words unspoken during their time apart would need to be said. Until then, they held one another, loved one another, and sank into sleep, in the comfort and security of one another.

A tear drifted down Evelyn's cheek to land on Daniel's face. She wiped the moisture away, surprised she hadn't felt them fill her eyes. Daniel opened his eyes and stared into hers. He lifted a hand to rest his palm against her damp skin. "I've waited and longed for this moment for four years. Can you ever forgive me?"

"Forgive what, Daniel?"

"I left."

Evelyn shook her head and pressed his hand closer. "I was never angry with you. I understood why you had to go."

"I don't deserve you, Evie, I never did, but God help me, I'll never leave you again." Their lips met and once again they lost their souls in each other. A few hours later, when they both awakened, the sun had reached higher in the sky and voices could be heard somewhere outside. No doubt news of Daniel's arrival had reached everyone. Many of them knew Daniel only as her husband, a man unknown. Others knew him briefly before his departure and called him friend.

They listened to the voices drift away, helped along by Tabitha and Harriett, both of whom Evelyn heard from where she guessed they stood on the porch, telling the others to leave the couple alone. Bless them, Evelyn thought.

"The town has grown some," Daniel said. "You've been busy. How's the timber?"

"It's a strong business, and we have the mine, too."

Daniel sat up and leaned back against the headboard. "A mine?"

"Yes." Evelyn nestled herself close to her husband while still facing him. "Do you remember Cooper, the guide who first brought us here?"

Daniel nodded.

"He found traces of gold in one of the river beds in '62. He swore there was gold to be found if we kept looking. He was right."

"Cooper found gold for you?"

"Not just for me, for the town. I financed everything and . . . told Cooper if we struck gold, he'd get forty percent of the mine.

We did. He's given most of it back to the town, as have I. He insisted paying for the extra materials needed to shore up the mine to make it safer after a harsh winter. A sheriff's office and medical clinic were built, though I've only recently written advertisements for those positions."

Daniel's expression left Evelyn worried for a few seconds. "Are you upset?"

He covered her hands and drew her close. "No, my dear. I have no right to be upset with anything you've done. Should you ever commit the gravest of sins I would still love and admire you. What you've accomplished . . . I should have been here."

"You're here now," she said, sinking against his bare chest. "You're here now and nothing else in this moment matters."

A few minutes of comfortable silence filled the air before Daniel said, "You and Cooper . . . have become friends."

Evelyn sat up, but remained close, her fingers entwined with his. "Good friends." She smiled and brushed the back of her hand over Daniel's chin. "He is as close to me as my sister, and just as dear."

Daniel smiled in return. "I sounded jealous."

"Perhaps a little. All I am and all I have has remained yours, and only yours."

Daniel hugged her close and pressed a kiss to the top of her head. "You haven't asked about what happened."

Evelyn had noticed the other scars. The one on his jaw must have bled terribly, but there were others she saw when he'd been in his bath, and a few her fingers touched on his back when they were in bed. He kept his life, his limbs, and his sanity. In her eyes, he was perfect.

"You'll tell me, when you're ready. I don't imagine the years are ones you want to relive anytime soon."

"Nothing in my previous life ever prepared me for what I witnessed on those battlefields. The fighting wasn't the worst part, though. It was the in-between. The quiet days and nights when we had only the cold and damp for company, and too much time to think of what we'd left behind."

Evelyn pressed her lips to his, held him close. "I will be right here, when you're ready, or if." She fidgeted with the sheet for a few seconds and said, "A few weeks ago I received a letter from Abigail. She said your name wasn't on any of the reports of dead or missing or hospitalized. Where were you?"

Daniel exhaled and closed his eyes briefly.

"I made a promise to someone, Evie. I gave him my word that if we both survived the war, I would help him find his family."

"I don't understand why—"

"I also promised him I wouldn't tell anyone, not even you, not until I was here and he was safe. Every day when I should have been traveling here, when I didn't write, I warred with my conscious, but I gave him my word."

"He must have been a very good man to be worthy of such a promise."

"Gordon Wells was his name. He was a slave, and he saved my life."

Tears once more filled Evelyn's eyes. She made no sound while she studied her husband's face. "Then he has my undying gratitude and devotion. Did he find his family?"

"He did. His son had died. He'd been traded away from the plantation where the family had slaved. His wife and daughter escaped   six   months   before   Lincoln's   Emancipation

Proclamation incited more escapes. Gordon lived in a loyal slave state, exempt from the proclamation. He thought if he stayed, his owner might not try to find Gordon's wife and daughter."

"Did it work?"

"For a time. His owner became ill and the overseer left. He made a deal with Gordon; he wouldn't send anyone after his family if Gordon remained until the end of the war."

"I don't understand."

"His owner was a desperate man by that time, having lost too many slaves."

"But Gordon—"

"Is honorable. He didn't try to explain his reasons for agreeing, and I didn't ask. I understood because in his situation, I would have done the same thing—to save you."

Evelyn brushed away a tear and leaned closer to her husband. "However did you two meet?"

"I was caught past Rebel lines on a scouting mission. I'd been shot near the plantation where Gordon lived. He found me in the river, pulled a bullet from my shoulder, and hid me until I was well enough to travel."

Evelyn touched the scar on Daniel's shoulder. "He sounds like a good man."

"I told him there would be a place for him, if he chose to come this far west."

Daniel had changed in the four years away. He'd always been a good man, a kind man, but Evelyn sensed in him a higher calling now. She believed herself untouched from the conflict, yet without her husband, she'd been forced to discover a side of herself previously unrealized.

Evelyn left the bed, slipped into her white linen robe, and

walked to the window. Their bedroom faced the back of the house, away from prying eyes and open to a meadow and the mountains beyond. "It's this town, Daniel. Your dream, what you imagined this place could become, that's what kept me going. I felt you by my side every day. Even in this last week when I feared never seeing you again, I felt you in me. I'm not one for fanciful talk, yet I know this valley is blessed. We've endured much and we're stronger for it."

She turned back to him. "These mountains brought me comfort, this house, knowing it was ours, made me feel safe, and these people . . ." She returned to him. "The people gave me purpose. I thought of returning to Pennsylvania a few times, especially in those early days, but I couldn't leave them. I couldn't leave the home we'd built together."

Daniel pressed his forehead against hers, his arms wrapped around her. "And we'll continue to build. Whitcomb Springs may have started as my dream, but it became your legacy. I want to help you carry that legacy into the future."

Evelyn held his hands close to her lips, brushed a kiss against his warm skin. "The legacy is ours. Always and forever ours."

They talked and dreamed, shared hopes and plans, as they lay together with the mountain breeze brushing over them through the open window. Tabitha and Harriett left them alone, and though Evelyn wondered where they stayed, likely at the hotel, she didn't worry about them. From this moment on, adversity would have no power to defeat them. Trials and joy awaited in equal measure, yet Evelyn's heart overflowed with hope and wonder. When night descended and Daniel's stomach rumbled, Evelyn smiled and he chuckled. She said, "I'm a fair hand in the kitchen these days. It's time you were fed again."

"You've fed me well, with more love than I ever imagined. Are you ready for the next chapter of our story?"

"With you beside me, I am ready for anything." She grinned, a wildly happy grin that hinted at teasing. "Even if that *anything* includes Abigail. She has a notion to come to Montana."

Daniel leaned against the pillows, playing like a man in grave pain. "Heaven help us now."

Evelyn pulled a pillow out from under his head and hit him with it. Together they laughed and rolled in the tangle of sheets. Even though she believed somber days lay ahead as Daniel found his way back into the world, today their lives brimmed with only the glow from their combined joy.

FORSAKEN TRAIL

Cooper McCord enjoyed a solitary life. When he first showed
Daniel and Evelyn Whitcomb the beautiful mountain valley in
Montana, he didn't expect to stay. After the Civil War began,
Cooper remained close and helped build the town, not realizing
he was building a home for himself. When an unexpected arrival
to Whitcomb Springs makes him question his reclusive life, will
Cooper retreat to his wilderness or allow himself to take a chance
and risk happiness?

FORSAKEN TRAIL

SHE NEVER IMAGINED dying at the hands—or paws—of a bear. Either she'd end up dead like the poor driver she hired in Bozeman or find a way to escape unscathed. Considering the layers of skirts and petticoats she wore, Abigail wasn't going to bet on her ability to outrun the great animal.

She remained still in the low branches of a tree. Unable to climb higher unless she removed her skirts, Abigail controlled her breathing so as not to alert the animal. The past few years of her life had been in pursuit of an education. Her work in the war relief had kept her busy for four long years, but she found time in the evening hours to consume knowledge. The more she learned, the more she wanted to know.

Abigail read most of the leather-bound volumes of work in her family's library, from philosophy to geography to history, and everything in between. Unfortunately, not a single text had explained what to do when confronted by five hundred pounds of bear. Magnificent though the animal was, Abigail didn't want to become dinner.

Poor Mr. Tuttle had fallen from the wagon and broken his neck when the horses spooked and ran off. She'd been unable to drag him away, let alone pull him up a tree. Even now, she watched as the massive brown bear sniffed around the body. She dispelled a deep breath when she realized it wasn't going to eat Mr. Tuttle. It looked around instead, smelling the air.

Abigail swore it stared directly at her. Too late, she recalled that bears climb trees. Her first thought had been to escape, and unable to outrun the creature, she went up. She calculated if the bear stood on its back legs, it could reach the low-hanging branches where she hid and knock her from the tree with one swipe. She grabbed the nearest branch above her head and pulled herself up. Abigail ignored the loud rip in her skirt and the sudden gush of cool air that hit her legs and climbed higher. Two more branches put her out of swiping distance.

The grizzly sauntered toward her and stood, staring and studying. She imagined it thinking of all the ways it could rip her apart and savor her like a delicious meal. The stays on her corset would be no match for those great claws, and the teeth . . . Abigail shuddered and reminded herself that most living creatures weren't vicious by nature.

Abigail knew the animal was aware of her location. It landed back on all fours and approached the base of the tree. The heavy breathing and snorting filled the silence.

"I don't suppose we can work something out?" she called down to the bear, feeling foolish but not knowing what else to do. "Why don't you go your way and I'll go mine?"

Abigail covered her ears and pulled herself as close to the tree trunk as possible. The bear turned its head toward the sound of the gunfire before dropping on all fours. Another bullet hit the tree near the bear's head. The bear snorted again and after the third shot hit the ground a few feet away, the animal turned away from the tree and headed across the clearing to the forest. Abigail kept her tight hold on the branches and didn't look down when she heard the sound of a horse beneath her.

"If you can manage to climb back down, he's gone."

"Yes, but now you're here." Abigail thought she heard a chuckle. She dared a glance but couldn't see much of the man's face, shadowed by his hat.

"I can ride away if you prefer, ma'am, but there isn't another soul likely to come by today." After a minute of silence, she heard a loud sigh. "If you aren't coming down, the least you can do is explain what happened to Tuttle."

"You know—knew—Mr. Tuttle?"

The man below her didn't answer right away. She heard movement and saw he was no longer on his horse.

"I did. Looks like a broken neck."

She squeezed her eyes shut and asked, "Did the bear . . . make it worse?" She dared not ask if the bear tore the poor man apart.

Silence.

"Sir?"

Another chuckle. "No one calls me sir, ma'am. The bear probably figured Tuttle wasn't going anywhere. He was more interested in finding out what crawled up the tree."

"I didn't crawl!" Abigail realized the ridiculousness of her situation and studied the branches beneath her. The climb down wasn't too far. One of her petticoats was caught on a protruding branch. She shifted and the delicate fabric ripped even more. "I don't suppose you'll tell me the truth, but if I come down, will you promise not to harm me?"

"Interesting question seeing as how if I wanted to harm you, I'd've come up after you by now or shot you out of the tree straight away. The bear was more dangerous, and I gallantly, if I may add, chased the bear away."

"That's hardly reassuring." Abigail thought she'd kept her mumbling quiet enough for him not to hear, but she heard that damnable chuckle. "If you'd be so good as to move away, *sir*, I'll climb down."

"Go ahead."

Abigail lowered a foot to the next branch down, found her footing, and shifted her weight until she stood entirely on one branch. Only a few more to go, she told herself, unaware until now how far she had climbed up. She searched for the torn petticoat still caught, slipped, and fell before the shriek left her lungs. She landed with a soft thud, arms wrapped around her, and tangled skirts in her face. "Put me down!"

"Yes, ma'am."

Once on solid ground, Abigail stumbled away from her rescuer. She brushed hair from her face that had fallen from her once neat coiffure and straightened her skirts to preserve modesty. She saw only her outer skirt was torn, and most of her petticoat still intact. "I apologize. It was unkind of me to be ungrateful when you went to so much trouble . . ." Her eyes met his.

She imagined a woman in one of the silly romance stories her mother enjoyed. Heart fluttering, nearly out of breath, and eyes enraptured by the dashing gentleman. Only this wasn't a story and there was nothing dashing about the stranger before her. Dangerous, rugged, and beneath the days' worth of beard, a handsome man. She wondered if he kept his hair long to protect from the elements or detract from his striking features. Could a man be beautiful, she wondered? His blue eyes fascinated her so much she looked up to the sky to confirm they were the same color.

"Ma'am?"

"Excuse me, sir. I meant to express my gratitude. There is no excuse for my poor manners. You rescued me from that bear and I am in your debt." Abigail stepped forward, showing some of the moxie her sister possessed in abundance, and held out her hand.

When the stranger didn't reciprocate, she dropped her hand to her side. "My name is Abigail Heyward, and Mr. Tuttle was escorting me to Whitcomb Springs."

COOPER STARED AT the outstretched hand, gloved in white lace, now torn and dirty, with long and delicate fingers. He noticed beneath the fabric her skin was soft, like her face. His eyes moved to take in everything from her black, laced boots and torn skirt to the fallen tendrils of honey-colored curls. He had let go of her too soon, by her startled request, though he would have liked to have kept her close a while longer. Six long years since he last held a woman close, and this one stirred things inside him like no other had.

Shame she was Evelyn's sister, and in his mind, untouchable.

"Cooper McCord." He walked toward his horse and mounted.

"You're not leaving me here?"

"Correct, Miss Heyward. I promised your sister that I would see you safely to Whitcomb Springs, but I imagine Tuttle brought you up here on a wagon. If you'll wait here a few minutes, the horses won't have gone far."

"Wait!"

The gentlemanly thing to do would have been to take her into town and come back for the body, but he refused to leave a good man dead for scavengers to take turns at his corpse.

"Miss Heyward?"

"You know my sister?"

Cooper nodded. "After you sent that telegram from Chicago, I offered to fetch you, seeing as how I had business in Bozeman. Learned you'd already hired someone, but no one remembered who." He saw her digesting what he'd already said. "You should have expected your sister would have sent someone."

"I arrived earlier than planned and was impatient to reach town. Mr. Tuttle was for hire."

"He is at that, but not much of an escort." He started walking away again when her next words stopped him.

"May I come with you? I see how wrong it is to leave Mr. Tuttle here alone, but . . ."

Cooper studied her, knowing it wasn't wise to get too close. He watched her eyes, filled with apprehension, and wondered what made her decide to trust him. He held out his hand. She remained by the tree, and he said, "Stay or go with me, Miss Heyward, but I'm riding, not walking."

He watched her look at the covered body and make her decision. She inhaled and straightened her back, though he doubted it could get any straighter than before, and walked toward him. She clasped his hand and looked up.

"If you can manage, you put a foot in the stirrup." Her incredulous expression told him that wasn't going to happen. Without asking permission, he reached down, grasped her underneath the arms, and pulled her into his lap. He ignored her startled reaction and waited for her to get settled.

He considered embarrassing her by mentioning the bright rosy hue rising in her cheeks, then thought better of it. The last thing he needed was to be too friendly.

"You followed us, I mean the wagon, back from Bozeman? I'm surprised we didn't meet on the road."

"I didn't come down the main road. There's a faster route, but it's not suited to wagons."

She leaned forward, separating her back from his chest, and he shook his head. Abigail said, "Evelyn and Daniel must trust you a great deal."

"They do." He left it at that and invited no further conversation. Cooper followed the wagon tracks with ease. The horses stopped in a meadow and grazed on spring grass. He saw no signs of predator tracks and counted the horses lucky. A quick inspection of the harness revealed one had loosened and a strap caught around one of the horse's legs. Blood trickled down over the animal's hoof. Cooper swore and dismounted. The other horse was uninjured but couldn't pull the wagon by itself, not weighed down as it was with two large trunks and two small trunks. Mr. Tuttle had secured them well with ropes and they had remained intact.

"Is she going to be all right?"

"Should be." He pointed to the trunks in the back. "Doesn't appear you lost anything."

"Possessions hardly matter when a man has lost his life."

Cooper studied her again, this time with admiration for more than her looks. On the outside, she appeared to be the beautiful, well-born eastern lady Evelyn had described, but Cooper wondered if there might be more beneath the genteel exterior.

He remembered the first time he guided Daniel and Evelyn Whitcomb into these mountains. A year before war divided friends and family, the Whitcombs traveled west for adventure and a beginning. He mistook Evelyn for a pampered woman unable to fend for herself. When her husband joined the Union army, she proved him and everyone else wrong.

Cooper stayed close by while she continued to build a town and help people search for their own new beginnings. He might have found her attractive in the beginning, but it was her strength and determination he admired most. They'd become loyal friends who respected each other, and later close as brother and sister without the bond of blood.

What his body and mind experienced when he looked at Abigail was different, with no thought of friendship or brotherly feelings. Lust, attraction, and now confusion thwarted his more common sensibilities. He'd left a big city long ago because of a well-bred and spoiled woman, and he'd be damned to let his heart risk breaking over another one.

He tried to keep his thoughts off Abigail. He took care with the injured animal. He unharnessed the mare and hitched his own horse up to the wagon. A strong gelding, the horse stood a few hands taller than Tuttle's other mare, but there was no other option if Cooper was to get Tuttle and Evelyn's sister to Whitcomb Springs. He removed the semi-clean cloth from around his neck, wet it with fresh water from the canteen, and tied it around the mare's injured leg to help stop the blood flow. The animal needed rest and treatment, but Cooper didn't think it would go lame. He secured the mare to the back of the wagon and turned to Abigail.

"It's time to go." He regretted the curt tone as soon as he said the words.

"Are you angry with me?"

Cooper smoothed the lines on his face. *Had he looked angry?* "Not at all. I don't like to see any animal in pain. My apologies."

"Is that why you didn't kill the bear?"

His eyes narrowed as he faced her. "The bear might have tossed you about some if it got the chance, but more often than not they'd rather steer clear of people. It gave me no reason to kill it."

They sat in silence on the wagon bench while Cooper turned the team back to the road. He told himself not to look at her, to ignore her, but a proper upbringing would not be squelched, no matter how he chose to live his life. "Your sister was surprised when she received your last message."

He sensed Abigail's surprise, and she confirmed it when she said, "I sent a telegram. Surely she received it right away."

Cooper smiled. "We don't have a telegram just yet. Telegrams go into Bozeman or Butte, and depending on who it's for, it comes up by the mail wagon or a rider. Seeing as how a lot of folks know about Evelyn's generosity, they sent a rider."

"You know her well, using her Christian name."

"She's been Evelyn to me for a long time now."

"And her husband?"

Cooper did glance her way this time. Her body went rigid and her voice hard. "Don't go thinking what you're thinking, Miss Heyward. Your sister and her husband are my friends. I've known them a long time."

"Evelyn mentioned you in her letters."

"Which explains why you decided to trust me, after I told you my name."

Abigail nodded. "The family worried about her when Daniel left. She spoke of you fondly."

"She's a good woman. They're good people, Evelyn and Daniel."

"She also said you were a tracker and miner."

Cooper guided the horses around a rock in the road and made a mental note to return and clear it off the path. The road to Whitcomb Springs narrowed in some areas and widened in others. It went uphill and down and overrun with grass in places, but Cooper and others from town kept it passable for horses and wagons.

"I'm a lot of things, Miss Heyward."

"You don't sound or look like a mountain man."

He grinned and gently slapped one of the leather reins on the rump of the mare. "And you've met many mountain men, to know what they sound and look like?" Cooper admired the way her cheeks pinkened.

"No, I haven't. I've read stories, but I suppose it's not the same thing."

He remained silent as he recognized the place where Tuttle's body lay waiting.

"Are you a mountain man?"

"Like I said, I'm a lot of things." Cooper pulled the horses to a stop so the back of the wagon was near the body and stepped down. "You ought to stay up there, Miss Heyward, while I rearrange things in back for Tuttle." She did as he suggested. Cooper glanced her way every so often to make sure she looked anywhere except the body. Abigail Heyward had more gumption than he would normally credit a city woman. She hadn't fainted, screamed, or wept.

"You can leave my things here," she said without turning around. "It doesn't seem right for Mr. Tuttle to ride with my luggage."

When he had Tuttle situated in the back alongside her trunks, Cooper climbed back onto the seat next to her. "Tuttle would have been disappointed, considering the trouble he went making sure your trunks were safe."

"You say he was your friend, yet you don't appear upset by his death."

Cooper set the horses in motion, keeping a slow and easy pace for the sake of the injured mare trailing behind them. "Who's to say how I feel. I liked Tuttle well enough. He was a good man but an irritable sort. He was also drunk when he fell off the wagon, so I figure his death wasn't anyone's fault except his own."

"He was drunk?"

Cooper nodded, and they started on a gentle incline. "Smelled it on him. He held his liquor pretty good, but he knew better than to take a lady on a wagon ride before he sobered up." He noticed her alabaster cheeks turn rose again. "Something you're not saying, Miss Heyward?"

"I offered Mr. Tuttle a good sum to depart early. He said it would take a day, perhaps more, yet I was impatient. His death was my fault."

They reached a plateau and Cooper halted the horses. "It's not your fault. Tuttle knew better, you didn't. No sense in believing otherwise. Truth be told, it was bound to happen with him." He put the team back in motion and they rambled along. "He'll get a proper burial, Miss Heyward, and that's all he'd care about in the end."

"I give you leave to call me Abigail, please. Miss Heyward sounds far too formal for this wilderness."

Cooper repeated her name a few times in his mind and enjoyed the way it rolled off his tongue. "If you don't mind, I prefer Miss Heyward." He saw the flash of disappointment in her eyes and admired her all the more for not saying anything about it. No doubt in his mind, Abigail Heyward was trouble. The sooner he delivered her safely to her sister and brother-in-law, the better.

ABIGAIL DRIFTED BETWEEN frustration and gratitude. Those feelings shifted entirely to concern when Cooper stopped the wagon and said they couldn't go on.

"What do you mean?"

He pointed, and she looked ahead. A massive tree lay in the center of the road. On either side boulders taller than a man prevented passing. "Do we have to turn back?"

Cooper shot her a look, and she said, "Yes, I know, a foolish question. Obviously, a tree that size must take a great number of men to move. Is there another way around?"

"There is. As I mentioned before, I didn't come down this way so I did not see the downed tree on the road."

He jumped down and led the horses off the road. She waited while he hefted and carried large rocks from nearby and set them behind each wagon wheel. When he finished, he started to remove the harness from the horses.

"Mr. McCord. I don't mean to be difficult, and I'm sure you have far more important matters to attend than seeing me to town, which I truly appreciate, but what are you doing?"

"Unhitching the horses, Miss Heyward."

I'm not going to ask. I'm not going to ask. She asked anyway. "And why are you unhitching the horses? If there is a way around—"

"We can't take the wagon the way we're going. Once I get a few men from town, we'll clear the road and I'll see your things are delivered."

"I don't care about my trunks, at least not too much. What about Mr. Tuttle, and the injured mare?"

"I'll bury Tuttle in a shallow grave, cover him with your trunks and the wagon, and bring him back to town after we move the tree. The mare can travel where we're going. The trail is passable but not wide enough for a wagon."

He sounded blasé, and she wondered what sort of man treated life and death with such a matter-of-fact approach.

When Cooper came around to her side of the wagon and offered to help her down, Abigail relented. Out of her element. That's what Evelyn would say, *did say* when she wrote back trying to convince Abigail not to make the journey west. Evelyn pleaded with her to wait until she and Daniel could meet her in St. Louis and travel the remaining miles to Montana. Abigail, in her impatience, set out with two cousins who were on their way to Chicago. She hadn't lied to them exactly though she failed to mention Chicago wasn't her final destination. As soon as she sent the telegram to Evelyn, she departed Chicago.

She trusted Cooper McCord. Even if her sister had not spoken of him with high regard, she sensed somehow she could trust him.

"The mare can't carry any weight, so your belongings will have to stay with the wagon. I have room in my saddlebags for a few items you might want to take along now."

Abigail thought of the piles of clothes, books, and treasures she'd tucked away when she left home.

He interrupted her thoughts with a question. "How long are you planning to visit your sister? Appears by your luggage you plan to stay a spell."

"I don't know yet, Mr. McCord."

He hauled her trunks, one by one, from the bed and set them aside. It was then she saw Mr. Tuttle. "You don't want to be looking at him."

"I've seen dead men before."

He leaned on the back of the wagon and studied her.

She felt exposed beneath his gaze, yet unable and not wanting to make him stop.

"Where?"

"At the hospital. Men and boys sent home. Some survived, but many failed to recover from their injuries. I read to them, fetched water . . . they deserved much more than I gave."

"Your sister knew about this?"

Abigail shook her head and tore her attention away from the body. "No. Neither did our mother. My father caught me once but kept my secret."

"Why did you do it?"

"I needed to do . . . something. I'm not brave, Mr. McCord. I was no Florence Nightingale or Clara Barton in the heat of battle tending wounds and saving lives. I was grateful to live in the North, removed from the worst of the fighting. Many of our acquaintances enlisted and never returned home. I remained safe at home, praying for the war to end, for our lives to return to normal." Abigail turned and stared at the mountains all around her. "When it was over, I realized nothing would be the same, not for me. I couldn't go back to balls and parties, dress fittings and lavish dinners. I want to have a purpose."

"And so, you came here."

Cooper whispered the words, yet Abigail heard them and realized how much she had revealed.

"HOW LONG WILL it take to reach town?"

Cooper secured the worn leather bags to his saddle, thinking of the trek ahead. "We'll be there tomorrow morning."

"But you said Whitcomb Springs wasn't far from here."

"It's not, but it's already late in the day. Storm's coming and I'd as soon get you to town before it reaches us. The trail leads us out of the way a bit and curves back around toward town. There's a place to wait out the storm." Cooper walked to her and stopped next to her and the horse. "Do you know how to ride?"

"Very well, Mr. McCord. Though, I'll admit to a lack of education for—"

"Trail riding?"

"Yes. The rolling hills of home do not compare to your rugged mountains. Are you certain . . . never mind. We should be on our way, yes?"

Cooper watched her in fascination. He guessed she wanted to ask if they could stay with the wagon, but she didn't cry and demand him to make things easier for her. When she grabbed the saddle horn and attempted to pull herself, Cooper stepped up beside her and lifted her into the saddle. He said nothing and neither did she. He thought the silence was better while he attempted to sort out the mixed feelings he had about escorting her to town. He swung up onto the back of his gelding and looked at Abigail, who stared at him. She didn't look away.

"The mare will follow us. Keep a good hold on the reins but keep it loose, too. If she veers off the trail for any reason, you bring her back in line."

"Is the trail dangerous, Mr. McCord?"

"Everything here is dangerous, Miss Heyward."

"I do wish you would call me Abigail. We're quite alone, which is already improper according to the standards by which I was raised. If proper is your concern—"

"It's not." Cooper smiled and shook his head at her. "You have a nice way of speaking." He sighed and looked at the trail ahead of them. "When we get to town, you're Miss Heyward again." He kept his gaze on her until she nodded her agreement. Cooper could avoid saying her name altogether. Better to keep his distance than dream for the impossible.

An hour on the trail and Abigail wondered how Cooper knew where they were going. The horses plodded along, surefooted and relaxed, through tall grass. Every once in a while, Abigail spotted what could be a trail beneath them, before it quickly disappeared under more grass, fallen twigs, and pebbles. Her traveling companion remained silent except to occasionally glance back and see how she was doing. Surprisingly well, she thought to herself, though aloud she assured him she was fine.

When she realized the trail they followed led into a forest thick with trees that blocked out much of the sunlight, Abigail asked, "How often is this trail used?"

"Not often."

Frustrated, she tried again. "And you say it's passable all the way to Whitcomb Springs?"

"Last I checked."

Patience, Abigail. Patience is your friend. She recited the mantra a few times when he stopped the horses, startling her. The mare she rode stopped without direction from her and was content to munch on grass. "Why have we stopped? The horses?"

"Horses are fine."

"Then—"

"We'll be moving along again shortly." He reached into a saddlebag and pulled out what appeared to be dried meat. He dismounted and walked it back to her. "This should hold you over until we break for camp."

She accepted the offering and stared, dumbfounded. "Camp?"

Cooper took his time getting back on his horse. She saw him focus on the ground and then up in the direction they'd come.

"There's a meadow and a small trapper's cabin we'll reach before dark. It doesn't get used much, and it's not what you're used to, but it will keep the rain off and the critters out."

Abigail grew increasingly frustrated with her guide. She told herself that if he hadn't come along, the bear might have mauled her. If he hadn't offered to escort her to town, she'd be left in the elements with poor, dead Mr. Tuttle until someone else happened along. No, she was grateful and wouldn't complain.

Abigail put all her trust in Cooper and followed him into the dark forest. She was surprised to discover peace and beauty within the darkness. Smatterings of light filtered through the thick branches and dew reflected the filtered rays. The fresh smell of pine and moss mixed with air purer than anything she'd breathed before was incredible. She relaxed and enjoyed the quiet, for even with Cooper and the horses close by, Abigail felt as though nothing else existed in her serenity.

The silence grew maddening. "Does the trail have a name?"

"Forsaken Trail."

"Sounds ominous."

He shifted, looked over his shoulder at her. Every time he did, she wanted to study him a little longer than his quick glances allowed. His voice comforted her, and as serene as her surroundings were, the silence became difficult.

As though he understood her problem, he said, "It was named by the Salish, or so it's been said. The story tells of a warrior who had won many battles against other tribes, but who also lost many of his own people in those same battles. He wandered the land, crossing tribal boundaries in an attempt to create peace among them.

"He fell in love with a Shoshone woman and returned to his people's land. They wouldn't accept her and he came here to these mountains. They lived alone. It is said he hunted this trail and made his home in the meadow. He named the trail to remember all those he lost, who bled into the earth, into the forsaken places where they never should have been."

Abigail pulled slightly on the reins to stop the mare, bringing Cooper's attention to her. "We need to keep going."

"Is the story true?"

"Most legends begin with some truth. You do not need to cry for them, Abigail. They have shed enough tears." He faced forward again and set his gelding in motion. The mare immediately followed, and Abigail remained silent, her thoughts on the Salish warrior and his wife, and on the quiet emotion she heard in Cooper's voice when he spoke of them.

Cooper led them from the forest a few hours later and into a meadow. They'd stopped only once. Abigail disliked having to ask for that much consideration, but Cooper didn't appear to mind. Never had she met a more accommodating man. Most men of her acquaintance played the part of gentleman with practiced and precise skill. Cooper's manner and kindness came naturally, honestly, with no pretense.

When they stopped in front of the trapper's cabin—a shack with a lean-to attached to one side—Abigail wasn't sure she could dismount. Her stiff muscles ached when she shifted. Cooper had warned her not to ride sideways on a western saddle, but she refused to ride astride. Now she regretted her pride for propriety's sake.

Before she slid off, Cooper was next to her, lifting her down. Once her feet met the earth, his hands lingered on her waist for a few seconds longer than necessary. Neither of them spoke, and he left her standing there while he tended to the horses. The emotions he evoked were both confusing and real.

"Abigail."

She turned, surprised that he used her given name. Despite her permission and request, he hadn't used it since they left the wagon. "Yes?"

"I need to get the horses settled in for the night. You can go on and see if anything can be used. I've left a few things here from time to time."

Curious, Abigail pushed open the wooden door and stood outside while light and air entered the small room. Grateful for the foresight not to walk in right away, she peered inside. Dust covered every surface and cobwebs hung from corners. A drab canvas hung from one of the two narrow windows, and neither had glass in their frames. She imagined such a place didn't need glass windows. She took a tentative step inside and scrutinized the rest of the interior, what there was of it, and determined that she may rather sleep outdoors.

"It's been longer than I figured, since anyone has been here."

Abigail pressed a hand to her chest and spun around. Though no one else could have gained access to the cabin without Cooper's knowledge, she was still startled by his sudden appearance. "You move without making a sound."

He shrugged. "A necessary skill for living in these mountains."

"Evelyn wrote that you lived primarily in town, or nearby these past four years."

"True enough."

"And before then?" She doubted he was the type of man to open up about his past, but the more time she spent with him, the more inquisitive she became.

"Here and there." He crossed the room and tore the canvas from the window. "If you want to wait outside, I'll get this place cleaned up enough for sleeping."

Abigail looked around again. A single cot was pushed against one wall and a scarred table and one chair sat on the opposite side. "I wouldn't mind sleeping outside tonight."

She caught a grin that came and went on his handsome face. He said, "You ever sleep outside?"

"No."

He chuckled. "There's a storm coming and it will hit tonight. You can't be caught outside in the rain; your sister would never forgive me. The cot will do for you tonight, and I'll keep watch."

"Keep watch for what?" Cooper didn't answer, so she prodded. "Is there some danger I should know about?"

"Go ahead on outside and I'll call you in when it's ready."

Abigail wondered about the odd expression and wariness in Cooper's eyes when she left the cabin.

COOPER CARRIED IN two buckets of water, left over from the last rain, and wiped away as much of the dust as he could. The cabin was not a fitting place for Abigail Heyward to stay or sleep in, but she hadn't complained. Evelyn was strong and sure and brave—now. When he first guided her and Daniel into these mountains, he doubted she would survive the first winter. She surprised him by thriving. Cooper never figured out what prompted him to remain behind after Daniel went to war.

He waited for Evelyn to return home to her family, yet she stayed, and so did he. Year after year he expected her to give up. Instead, she planted her gardens, hired men from all over to slowly build up the town and carve out the road to allow for supply wagons and travelers. When he discovered gold in one of the creeks near town, she put her trust in him and opened the mine.

Evelyn found her courage and remained in Montana. He remembered the doubt and fear in her eyes, yet every day she grew stronger and less dependent on him. Abigail was like her sister. If he hadn't come along, he believed Abigail would have figured out how to get past the bear and find a way to Whitcomb Springs. Perhaps she saw more of the war than she'd confessed to her sister. He shook his head from thoughts of the war and stepped outside into the shafts of narrow sunlight. Clouds rolled in and he estimated another hour before the first part of the storm hit.

"Abigail?" He called her name a second time, louder. "Abigail!" He ran around the small cabin, finding no sign of her. He returned to the front and looked down. Dainty boot prints had pressed into the grass and soft earth, leading toward the trees. His heart rate increased, and he followed her prints, shouting her name. When he crossed most of the clearing between the cabin and trees, Abigail emerged with a smile on her face and her arms burdened with twigs. She looked perfect.

She moved toward him, so far unaware of his worried state. "I confess that I don't know anything about fires or if the stove inside works. I thought . . ." Her eyes met his. "What's wrong, Cooper?"

"Don't ever do that again."

"I didn't go far. You've done so much and I wanted . . . to help."

Cooper lifted the twigs and branches from her arms. "You don't know what you're doing. It's not safe out here on your own. Once you're in town, you'll be your sister's problem. Until then, I'm responsible for you."

"You have no right to be angry with me." He heard Abigail following him as he started for the cabin. She continued to speak even though he didn't respond. "I'm grateful for you coming along when you did, Mr. McCord, but I didn't ask you to be responsible for me. I could have stayed with the wagon and poor Mr. Tuttle until help came." Her boots pounded on the boards when she entered the cabin behind him. "It was not my intention to inconvenience you. Why did you bother with me?"

Cooper dropped the twigs and turned. "You're Evelyn's sister, and she's about the only family I have." He exhaled and told himself to calm down before he said anything else. "It wasn't safe to stay with the wagon. I wrapped Tuttle up the best I could, covered him with dirt and your trunks, but the critters are going to smell death and come looking. Anything from bears to wolves, and if they found us, they would have tried to make a bigger meal of us all."

Abigail blanched. "They're going to—" she stifled the reflex to gag "—eat him? Why did you leave him there? We could have put him on the other mare."

"The mare is barely going to make it to town. She can't take any weight, and I wasn't going to leave her wounded and unable to run away if wolves found her. Tuttle knew these mountains and his departed soul isn't going to think less of us for surviving."

Abigail lowered herself into the single chair. He hated seeing any woman scared. "We'll be in Whitcomb Springs tomorrow, then I'll return to the wagon with men and clear the road. It will be all right, Abigail."

"Would we really have been in danger, if we stayed with the wagon?"

"Yes." It was the simpler answer, easier. Cowardly. "I'm not taking any chances. We aren't too far from town, but if you plan on staying out here, even for a long visit, you have to understand the realities. You could walk through the meadow next to your sister's house and happen up on a mountain lion or bear. Worse, a stranger who won't give thought to your screams."

Abigail shuddered, and he saw her shrink back. "You're a very blunt man, but I see your point. I wasn't doubting your decision to keep moving. If I am to stay—"

"If?"

"*If* I am to stay, I need to learn how to survive. I appreciate your patience with my inexperience."

He watched her stand and leave the cabin. The first rumble of thunder shook the heavy air. He continued to watch her through the open door. She stared into the distance though he couldn't see her face. Were her eyes open? What was she thinking? He asked himself these and many other questions, knowing answers would not come tonight.

THE FIRST SIGN of rain dropped on Abigail's nose. She'd discarded her hat to watch the sun set over the trees. The need to feel the cool breeze flow through her hair outweighed decorum. The simple act released her, for a few seconds, from the burden she carried with her. The heavy load of doubt about leaving home and her reasons why. Her mother called her impulsive and her father made sure she had plenty of funds to see her on her journey and for the shopping she planned to do in Chicago, where they believed she went. By now, her cousins would have sent word to her parents. She hoped her letter to them reached Pennsylvania first.

A few more drops hit her head and a spark of lightning coursed through the darkening sky. Clouds opened to reveal a small section of the galaxy, to showcase her flickering stars. It lasted only a moment before the wind blew the curtain of clouds closed. She sensed him watching her with those unreadable eyes. Abigail glanced upward once more and returned inside where warmth from the stove drove away the cold. He stirred something in an indented pot on the small, black stove. The scent filled the cozy room and reminded Abigail how long it had been since she'd eaten a full meal.

"The beans are about ready. I didn't have anything else except this and jerky in my saddlebags, but it will keep your stomach full until we reach town tomorrow morning."

He continued stirring the beans, his back to her. She approached him, determined that he look at her when she spoke to him. "Cooper?"

He looked up.

"I'm sorry."

"Nothing to be sorry for."

Thunder blasted through the air once again, followed by another flash of lightning. "Will it reach us?"

Cooper appeared to listen and then shook his head. "We should be fine."

"What about the horses?"

"The lean-to will keep them dry."

She accepted the plate of beans and spoon he handed her and noticed he didn't take any for himself. "You're not eating?"

"You have your fill. I'm going to check on the horses."

Abigail waited ten minutes before checking the silver watch fob attached to her outer breast pocket. She never went anywhere without the watch, a gift from her father. Ten minutes turned to fifteen when the cabin door opened and Cooper walked in, soaked through.

"It's coming down hard out there, but the thunder has stopped. Horses are secure for the night so long as the noise doesn't return. Scout doesn't mind too much, but Tuttle's mares are a mite skittish."

"Scout?"

Cooper stoked the flames in the stove. "My horse."

He didn't seem inclined to hold up the conversation, keeping his back to her as he did. Abigail succumbed to exhaustion and glanced toward the cot. A blanket not there earlier now covered the dusty mattress. Another lay on the edge.

"You should be warm enough tonight with the fire going. Try to get some rest."

Abigail sank onto the cot and spread a wrinkle from the blanket. "Thank you, Cooper."

Cooper nodded once and settled in the chair at the table. To her surprise, he withdrew a knife and a small piece of wood shaved down in places. Too weary to do anything except lay down, Abigail spread out over the blanket and drew the second one over her body.

The storm abated and sounds of the evening forest drifted through the open windows. The horses nickered a few times before quieting. Cooper whittled at the piece of pine, slow, easy movements downward, turning a simple piece of wood into a replica of his horse. He wished he had the skill to carve Abigail's face. He moved his eyes every few seconds to study the soft lines of her cheek and the way her long eyelashes brushed the skin beneath her eyes. When an occasional soft moan escaped her lips, he would stop his hands and watch to make sure she was still asleep. He had nothing to offer a woman like Abigail Heyward.

For the first time since he left Boston ten years ago, a part of him wished he was still the type of man fit for such a woman. He'd met a few from larger cities who yearned for adventure and traveled to the open plains or high mountains, only to realize what they yearned for more than adventure was comfort and convenience. Evelyn was one of the first of her kind to stay and build a life in these mountains. Since she and Daniel founded Whitcomb Springs, others like her came and forged their version of new beginnings. He admired these women, yet still believed they were an exception.

ABIGAIL TURNED ONTO her back then faced him again, her eyes still closed. She moaned and cried out a name. "Jacob!" She swatted at the air around her for a second and appeared to calm down. Cooper was on his haunches next to the cot, there if she needed to be awakened. She thrashed, her arms connecting with his face. She said the name again, this time on a moan with tears cascading down her cheeks.

"Abigail, wake up." He held her arms so close so she couldn't hurt herself. "Please, Abigail. Wake up!" Cooper smoothed her hair back, and when he pulled away, his hand saw that it was damp from her sweat. He shook her gently until her eyes opened in a rush.

"Jacob!" She looked around as she exhaled one frantic breath after another. Her eyes met his and Cooper saw the exact moment when she realized he was real and she no longer suffered in the nightmare. "Cooper." She whispered his name and grasped his hand. "You're alive."

"I'm alive. I'm right here." He held onto her hand, never losing contact with her gaze. "You were having one heck of a nightmare."

She tugged at the top buttons of her travel jacket. He knew modesty prevented her from removing even her outer clothes before she fell asleep, but between the heat from the stove and the light wool of her fancy clothing, she appeared to be uncomfortably warm.

"I haven't had one in weeks. I'm sorry to . . . I'm sorry."

This is a bad idea, Cooper thought even as he wiped a few tears from her cheek. "Don't be sorry. Do you want to talk about it?"

Abigail shook her head and released his hand. He rose so she could scoot to the edge of the cot. "The storm has stopped."

Cooper nodded.

"Is it safe to go outside for a few minutes? I just . . . need a few minutes."

By way of an answer, he opened the door for her. "Call out if you need me. I left a couple of buckets out front to collect more rain water."

She thanked him and stepped outside. He closed the door behind her. Meager though their privacy was, she deserved as much as he could give her. Cooper wiped both hands over his face a few times. He stopped himself from going to one of the windows when he heard her footfalls on the wet grass and twigs. He gave in and crossed to the opening in time to see her walk toward bushes still in the first budding. Winter had been long and spring late, making everything in their corner of the mountains lush and full. He moved away when she ducked out of sight. Cooper returned to the chair and his whittling.

A short while later the splash of water out front alerted him of her return. He didn't know why, but he sensed that opening the door for her, coddling her, wasn't what she needed or wanted. He understood her struggle and recognized the look in her eyes when she woke from whatever demons tormented her sleep. She wasn't in Montana only to see her sister. Abigail left behind more than family and carried the pain with her still.

She opened the door and stepped inside, saying nothing. He followed her lead and kept silent, even when she removed her tailored traveling jacket and laid it on the end of the cot. She spread herself out once more but didn't close her eyes and fall asleep as Cooper hoped she would. Instead, she looked directly at him.

"Have you always lived out west?"

He swept his knife smoothly over the wood's surface, away from his face. The new shredding joined the others on the floor at his feet. "No."

"Where are you from?"

Cooper tried to gauge her mood. Smudges of dark skin appeared under her eyes, shadows he suspected were there long before she decided to leave Pennsylvania. If she needed to talk, to forget whatever haunted her, he'd reveal everything about himself, even if the thought of doing so made him cringe. "Boston."

Surprise flickered in her eyes, though not an insulting surprise, more curious. "I visited there once. Why did you leave?"

He'd come a long way from those years in the city. "For a lot of the same reasons most folks come west. I was young and longed for adventure. I finished school and was set on a path my father approved of, but one I didn't want, so I left."

"And what did your father want for you?"

"The family business. Import and export, neither of which interested me." Cooper turned back to his piece of pine wood, smoothing a thumb over the surface. He had a way to go before it would look like Scout.

"If you're from Boston, why didn't you return home to fight in the war?"

And there it was, the question he guessed she really wanted to ask all along. When he didn't answer right away, she apologized and mumbled a "never mind." Cooper placed the wood on the table and sheathed his knife in his boot. The room seemed to close in on him and he needed space. He moved to stand by one of the windows and let the fresh air course over him. The clouds had cleared, leaving a celestial wonder of stars to gaze upon. "When I first left Massachusetts, it wasn't enough to get a little way from my father and the family responsibility. I went as far as I could without boarding a ship."

"The Pacific Ocean?"

Cooper smiled. "Not that far, but close. I went to California and made my way north. The Oregon and Washington Territories were created, and not long after several conflicts with the native tribes broke out. I was foolish enough not to leave when I had the chance. I signed on as a civilian attached to the army. I kept records on everything that happened. As much as I wanted to leave, I had agreed to stay on until the end of the conflicts. I learned to shoot, hunt, track, and anything else that might help keep me alive. I wrote down every horrible thing each side did to the other, kept a journal of every man in the company who died, and did my best to keep a record of the other side's deaths."

Cooper sighed and gripped the rough edge of the window. "Hostilities broke out between the army and the Yakama people. A few deaths, broken treaties, rape, unruly prospectors, and the death of a man named Bolon of the Bureau of Indian Affairs, made a lot of people nervous. Both sides sensed an uprising and what followed . . . It took four years for them to sign a peace accord. What people are capable of doing to each other was something I'd never witnessed before that."

He turned around and faced her, leaning against the cabin

wall. She sat up now, her feet tucked under her legs and the blanket wrapped around her shoulders. "I saw enough death to last me ten lifetimes. I couldn't watch brothers, friends, and countrymen slaughter each other. Don't get me wrong, those who fought for the right reasons are good and noble men. What it makes me, I don't know."

THIS TIME THE tears in Abigail's eyes weren't for herself but for Cooper. She hadn't expected him to reveal so much. No one talked of the war back home, at least around her, claiming she was too gentle. They wanted to forget, to go back to the way life was before the spring of 1865 brought the beginning of an end. She fought an internal battle about her reasons for leaving home. She avoided her parents' questions and had left the truth out of her letters to Evelyn. Yet she believed this man, this stranger she'd known for less than a day, would understand.

As though reading her mind, Cooper asked, "Why did you really come to Montana, Abigail?" He recited her name with reverence, as though savoring each syllable. "Who's Jacob?"

She wrapped the blanket tighter around her body and exhaled a shaky breath. "He was a patient at the hospital where I volunteered. He was from Virginia, a prisoner far from home and alive, barely, because a Union surgeon showed enough compassion to treat his more serious injuries before helping Union soldiers who came in on the same wagon.

"He was so young, eighteen two months before. The war was almost over, but no one knew how close. He wanted to fight for his home so he joined. Two months later, he lay in the hospital. I read to him, sat with him when he was frightened, and wrote letters for him to his family. I don't know if they ever reached Virginia, but I promised him. He lived for two weeks, three days, and sixteen hours before he jumped out of a second-story window."

Abigail caught a movement and shifted her gaze to Cooper. He stood closer to her now but still kept a distance between them. She had to finish telling him, had to tell someone. "The Union doctor who operated on him and I were the only people there when Jacob was buried. No letter ever came back from his family. I learned after the war that their home had been burned, with them inside." Tears fell freely now.

Cooper cleared his throat before speaking. "You never told anyone."

She shook her head and swiped at the moisture on her face. Abigail tried to keep her body from shaking. "I mentioned how my father found out I volunteered at the hospital, but he didn't know I helped directly with the wounded. If he, or my mother, had . . . it's not that they're unkind, but they believed me too fragile. They were right." A shudder coursed through her body. When Cooper sat next to her and pulled her into his arms, she couldn't understand why until she recognized sobs coming from her. She gripped his arms and leaned into him, drawing from his heat, his strength, and their shared sorrows.

Abigail remained in his embrace until she had no tears left to cry. When she pulled back, their faces were a few inches apart, and she needed only to whisper. "You won't tell Evelyn, will you?"

She saw something akin to pain in Cooper's eyes when he answered. "No. You'll tell her in your own time, if you want to."

"Have you told anyone about those four years in

Washington?"

"Not until tonight."

Abigail thought he might kiss her. They only met, but she would have allowed him the liberty. Instead, he brushed his fingers over her jaw and moved away.

"Think you could sleep a little now? There's only a few hours until daylight."

She nodded and lay back down. She fell asleep, imprinting his every feature to her memory.

SUN FILTERED IN through the open windows and a few cracks in the walls, waking Abigail from the few hours of restful sleep she'd managed to get. Sharing with Cooper had soothed the ragged edges of grief. Only time would heal her tattered soul, but at least now she believed an end to the misery was possible.

The horses snorted and Cooper's gentle voice, the one that soothed her last night, calmed the animals. Abigail hurried to get up. She folded the blankets and made use of the water in the bucket Cooper must have brought in while she slept. When she opened the door, she found Cooper hunched next to the injured mare, his hand moving up and down her rear leg.

"How is she faring?"

He must have heard her come out because he didn't look up. "She should be okay. Might not carry weight again, but she'll live. The girl deserves a rest." When he stood, he faced her.

Cooper didn't bring up her middle-of-the-night confession and tears, and neither did she. "How long will we ride today?"

"A few hours."

He was back to being taciturn, offering only those few words in response. Cooper rested a hand on the back of the mare and stared at her. If she knew him better she'd think he was annoyed; her parents always found her endless questions a nuisance. But she didn't know him better.

Abigail unconsciously clutched a fist at her breast and looked around. "The mountain lion or the bear worried you last night, didn't they? You said you were going to keep watch."

"The animals go where they want. If one gets too close to town or livestock, we do what we have to, but I never hunt an animal for sport or because it's easier. Most of the time we can track it away from where we don't want them, but it doesn't mean they won't return." He patted the horse's rump and said. "We need to be heading out now."

Abigail nodded her understanding and started for the trees. "I will hurry. And Cooper? Is it always about life and death here?"

His eyes darkened and for a second, she thought she saw sadness in them. "It's life and death everywhere."

THREE HOURS OF silence later, Cooper led their small party of two, plus one extra horse, into Whitcomb Springs. He was a man of few words and he'd already said more than he ever had at one time to anyone. He wanted to bring up last night so many times. Instead, he kept quiet and allowed her to enjoy the magnificent scenery. Every once in a while, he glanced back to find her eyes closed and a smile on her lips as she tilted her face back to the sun.

She took his breath away and made his heart ache for wanting what he shouldn't want. He remembered his father saying something similar about Cooper's mother. Thaddeus McBride may have been a dictator of a father, but he loved his family and adored his wife. Cooper never understood how one woman could affect a man so deeply—until now. He managed to go through thirty-two years of life without love. He figured he could last another thirty-two. A man couldn't lose what he didn't have. Townspeople waved and shouted hellos as they passed. Cooper had been a fixture in the town since the first cabins and trading post were erected. He liked belonging somewhere and only realized it now as he looked upon familiar faces and welcoming smiles. Evelyn and Daniel likely told a few people of her sister's impending arrival. Still, they'd be curious about the trail-weary lady in the city clothes, speculate among themselves as to why she came west.

He turned them right on another road, passed the general store and hotel. The Whitcomb's house stood out above the rest, as tall as the hotel that rarely saw guests. Evelyn insisted on a hotel, not just a boarding house. She predicted one day enough folks would get in their heads to pass through their town.

"Cooper?"

He indicated to his horse, with a gentle tug on the reins, to hold back. When Abigail's mare came alongside his, they continued on.

"Is that Evie's house?"

Cooper smiled, recognizing the shortened name Daniel sometimes used when speaking of Evelyn. "Daniel made sure it was finished before he left."

Abigail looked around in amazement. "She imagined all of this?"

"She did. Stubborn lady, your sister. I have a feeling you take after her in that way."

Abigail turned to him and he grinned to let her know he was teasing. She returned his smile and for a moment they were happy just to be alive and together. When the front door of the house opened and Evelyn shouted her sister's name, the moment passed and Cooper dismounted. He walked around his horse and put enough room between the animals to help Abigail down. If his fingers lingered longer at her waist than they should have, she said nothing of it.

Evelyn hurried through the open gate and ran to her sister, pulling the shorter woman into a fierce and loving hug. "When I saw you from the window riding in, I couldn't believe it." Evelyn stepped back and directed her next question to Cooper. "How did this happen?"

Abigail drew her sister's attention. "I'll explain everything, Evie, I promise." She jumped a little with delight when she saw Daniel approach and embraced him as she would a brother. "You look like a farmer," she said with a wide grin.

"We're clearing more land to put in an orchard. How are you Abbie, girl?"

"Perfect."

Evelyn slipped an arm around Abigail's waist. "First thing, a bath, and then I want you to tell me everything. You, too, Cooper."

Cooper enjoyed witnessing the family reunion. He was an only child and never knew the bond of a sibling. He envied them. "I have to feed and water Scout then head back out. We left a wagon with Mr. Tuttle at the bend by the large oak." Cooper hated reporting a death. "Tuttle didn't make it. He was driving Miss Heyward here. It's a long story, but the telling of it will have to wait or be done without me. I need to get back and take a few men. A tree's blocking the main road, and we couldn't get the wagon through."

Evelyn's face bore various expressions from surprise to sadness all wrapped in a layer of curiosity. Daniel said, "I'll come with you, Cooper."

"Shouldn't you—"

"I'm coming."

Cooper guessed Daniel not only wanted to help, this being his town, but he'd get the story faster from him than if he waited for Abigail's retelling of events. "Appreciate it. I'll get a few more men and meet you at the blacksmith's. I have a horse here that needs tending."

When Cooper turned his horse around and started walking away, he heard his name. He also heard Abigail whisper something to her sister and Daniel. A second later she stood next to him.

"Were you going to say goodbye?"

"I'll be back tomorrow, Miss Heyward."

He saw the hurt in her eyes. He'd told her when they reached town she'd be Miss Heyward again. It had to be this way, he told himself.

She held out her hand. "Thank you, Mr. McCord." She added in a whisper, "For everything." Abigail returned to her sister and brother-in-law, and Cooper walked away without looking back.

AN HOUR LATER, after a warm bath and slipping into clothes Evelyn laid out on the guest bed, Abigail felt more herself. Evelyn stood three inches taller than her and the skirt hung a little low to the ground, but after what she'd been through to get her, clean rags would have sufficed. Abigail came downstairs to find her sister alone in the kitchen setting up their tea.

Evelyn set a teapot on the tray and glanced up. "You look more yourself. How do you feel?"

"Better, thank you." Abigail looked around at the beautiful home. It was a third the size of their family home in Pennsylvania, and Abigail adored it. It felt like a home rather than a showpiece. Their house had always been a happy place, at least before the war, but they'd never gone into the kitchens or attics, considered strictly servant domains. "If mother could see you now."

"She taught us to serve tea."

"Serve it once it was brought in and carefully arranged by a servant. You look wonderful, Evie. Happy. How marvelous it must be to have Daniel home."

Evelyn blushed and said, "Let's go into the parlor and enjoy our tea. The gardens are in their first bloom, and we can enjoy them more from there."

Abigail followed her sister into the cozy room with lots of light shining through the windows. She may not know what it takes to build a house, but Abigail recognized expensive when she saw it. Though modest compared to their upbringing, everything from the solid walls and thick carpets on the floors to the furnishings and china spoke of comfort and elegance. "This is what you've been spending your money on." She accepted one of the fine china teacups and sipped the hot tea. "I approve. So, would Mother and Father."

Evelyn said nothing until she fixed her own tea and took the seat opposite Abigail. "I considered easing into this conversation, but I find I cannot. You can't know how happy I am to see you, Abbie, but why the rush to leave home?"

"I told you I wanted to visit."

"Yes, later. When I received your note from Chicago, I almost wrote Mother and Father to find out what happened. It's a dangerous journey through the territories. However did you get so far on your own?"

Abigail prepared herself for the questions, and she wondered if Cooper and Daniel were having the same conversation as they rode to fetch poor Mr. Tuttle. She set her cup on the table between them. The fine Irish linen bore no stains or wrinkles. "How do you manage all of this on your own?"

"There are two women who help out inside and the gardens. Harriett is helping at the general store today and Tabitha is looking after a neighbor who has a sick child. Please don't change the subject, Abbie. I need to know what's happened back home. You lied to Mother and Father when said you were going to Chicago."

"I'm not putting you off, Evie. I needed time to find the courage to tell you."

"You've traveled thousands of miles. This should be the easy part."

"Not when you've heard everything." Abigail sat forward on the plush chair with its beautiful plaid cloth. "Mother and Father know by now. I wrote them when I was in Chicago. I will tell you all of it, but please don't interrupt and don't scold me until I've finished." Abigail spent the next thirty minutes repeating every event from the time she left their cousins in Chicago to how Mr. Tuttle died, the bear, Cooper finding her, and their journey up the trail to Whitcomb Springs. She told her all of it, except the private story about Jacob that she shared with Cooper or his own story. Those secrets she kept close and unspoken. "I love our parents, but they wanted to go back to the way things were before the war. So many friends of ours died and others returned crippled or depressed. I needed a change, Evie. Surely you understand."

Evelyn remained silent for several minutes, making Abigail nervous. She did not require her family's approval for her choices, but she and her sister had always been close, and Abigail despaired disappointing her. Chirping birds and the distant sounds of people going about their lives broke through the quiet. She enjoyed the view of the gardens and the mountains beyond the glass windows, covered in green pines and topped with snow. Abigail marveled at their height and beauty. She imagined waking up every morning to see those mountains and inhale the crisp air, which was nothing like the heavier, humid air back home. "I do understand. Have you told me everything?"

Abigail didn't want to lie. "No, but please accept there are things I'm not ready to tell you."

"Promise me that you'll tell me when you are ready. I know what it is to hold something inside. I was blessed those four years. You wrote me often and listened to my worries, and Cooper was here for me, when I needed to speak to someone."

"Yes, Cooper is a good friend."

Abigail shifted uncomfortably under her sister's quiet perusal, but no admonition came.

Evelyn said, "When you do write home again, be sure to leave out the tales of your recent adventures."

"I will." Abigail bore no regrets for the stormy night she spent tucked away in the cabin with Cooper. They both needed to share their sorrows, and in their giving of secrets, a bond, deep and lasting, had formed. The senseless loss of life on both sides still haunted him, just as Jacob's death haunted her. "He was a gentleman, Evie."

The statement required no answer, but Evelyn said, "Abigail, I don't mean to scold, and you'll come to learn that proper doesn't always have a place in this wilderness. In your situation, you did everything I would have. Cooper's only concern was for you. That's the kind of man he is."

"He's a good one, isn't he? Like Daniel."

Evelyn smiled, her eyes brightening with moisture. "Yes, like Daniel."

DANIEL RETURNED THE next morning after the men went to clear the road and fetch Mr. Tuttle. They buried him in the town cemetery next to the church by the creek. It was a peaceful place with views of the meadow and mountains beyond. When she'd asked if the animals left Mr. Tuttle alone, Daniel refrained from going into detail and Abigail decided she'd rather not know. When she mentioned Cooper must be busy, Evelyn gave her an odd look and said nothing. Three more days passed before Abigail saw Cooper again.

Abigail needed to get away from the house for a little while. She visited every business in town—the few open businesses— and let her sister explain their plans for growth. Evelyn told her they'd sent out advertisements for a doctor and sheriff, with many more responses for the sheriff position. Abigail imagined the difficulty of finding an educated and licensed doctor to leave a hospital or private practice to come so far away from cities and amenities. The tour of the town resulted in meeting a variety of wonderful men, women, and children, though she remembered only a few names.

Despite the small population, Abigail found herself in need of alone time. She wanted to explore on her own and promised Evelyn she would stay close enough for them to hear and see her. Abigail accepted her sister's protective nature, and at one time welcomed it. No longer. She'd witnessed too much to go back to being the naive girl sheltered from life's horrors. She followed the stream where she found the deer path Daniel had mentioned. The path continued along the flowing water until it widened into what her brother-in-law explained would eventually become a river feeding into a lake. Abigail wanted to see it all.

She happened upon a trio of deer grazing and made herself comfortable on a large boulder next to the stream bank. They looked up once and continued eating the lush grass, unperturbed by her presence. An unfamiliar sound came from above and Abigail tilted her head back to search the sky. An eagle, with a wing span she'd never seen before on a bird, soared above. It circled twice before flying away and landing in a distant tree. Abigail laid back on the rock, spread her arms, and stared into the cloudy sky. She longed to be free as the eagle.

COOPER CAME UPON her with her arms spread wide and the hint of a smile on her face. He'd gone first to the house, searching for her, begging Evelyn without words to not ask any questions. It was Daniel who pointed to where Abigail ventured, and soon he found her. He waited, allowing her the peace she obviously felt and needed. He struggled for three days wanting to go to Abigail, to explain why he left the way he had, and each day he stayed away. He withdrew from town when they brought Tuttle's body and wagon back. He watched the funeral from a distance, though his eyes remained focused on Abigail. Her fancy clothes suited her even if they were out of place in the wild surroundings.

Three days and he gave in, unable to keep away any longer. Whenever he closed his eyes, he saw all the men he watched die and many he helped bury. Only now, those images faded, to be replaced by the wounded look in Abigail's eyes when he left. No one had managed to churn his emotions the way she did. He had to see her at least once more.

He noticed the twig on the deer trail and stepped on it, bringing Abigail to a sitting position. Her eyes widened at first, but he was uncertain about what he saw next. Confusion? Joy?

"You stayed away."

Cooper covered the distance between them in a few strides. He removed his hat and sat down next to her on the boulder, facing her. "I shouldn't have."

"Why did you?"

The deer, disturbed by their voices, scattered across the meadow. "I needed time to think."

"You came back. Evelyn said you would."

"This is home. I'll always come back."

"Have you stayed away because of me? Daniel seemed surprise not to see you around."

"I come and go, more so since Daniel returned." His heart's beat increased every time he evaded the topic that brought him out here, searching for her. "I'm not good with words, Abigail."

She shifted slightly to look at him more directly. The move brought her hand closer to his. "You could try."

He chuckled and pointed to the eagle above. It left its perch and now flew over them toward the mountains. "I understand him better than I do people. The land, these mountains, the animals, make more sense to me than the words I've been trying to figure out how to say. I could try to say them, but I suppose they won't come out right."

Abigail pleased him when she slipped her hand under his and linked them skin to skin. "We knew each other for one day and one night. It's not enough time for anyone to know a person."

"No, it's not. I'd like to know you."

He sensed her trembling nervousness, and with his words she relaxed. "I thought you were going to say something else."

"I was." Cooper squeezed her hand. "I had planned to leave. I came to see you one last time, to say goodbye to Evelyn and Daniel."

"And to me?"

"No." With his free hand, Cooper took a risk and cupped her cheek against his palm. Her skin warmed beneath his touch. "I couldn't say goodbye to you."

"You said you planned to leave. And now?"

He smiled and dropped his hand to her other side. "And now I'm not. I'm not the man my father hoped I'd become. That man is someone who might have deserved you. I don't, but I sure as hell am going to do my best. I want to know you, Miss Abigail Heyward. That is, if you're staying."

Abigail leaned closer to him. "Evie and Daniel are likely watching us, but I don't care. I'm staying. I don't want to go back to an existence of parties and charities and dinners with people bejeweled in too much finery. Those days for me are gone. I experienced a lifetime in our day and night together and I want more of it. Yes, Cooper McCord, I'm staying. And I want to know you, too."

Cooper released a shuddering breath and brought Abigail's hand to his lips. "We have a lot of learning to do about each other."

She brought their joined hands to her heart. "We have time."

Unchained Courage

Daniel and Evelyn Whitcomb dreamed of adventure as they made a home in the Rocky Mountains. Four years after Daniel left Montana, he returns from the Civil War a man uncertain of where he belongs. Through courage, honor, and the arrival of an old friend, Daniel finds a way back to the life he once imagined. Join him in "Unchained Courage" for a lesson in the power of hope, faith, and remembrance.

UNCHAINED COURAGE

DANIEL LED HIS horse over the familiar two-mile ride up the mountain trail. He reached a small clearing, and in the center a lake spread out in glistening glory, reflecting the mountain peaks behind it. He dismounted and stared in awe at the vista as his speckled horse grazed. Images of Evelyn overlapped his vision until it seemed a transparent silhouette of her smiling face hovered over the mountains.

A well-kept cabin stood a dozen yards from the crystal-clear lake. The stream feeding into it from the north flowed out to the east and created a short waterfall down a slope of rocks. Cooper McCord, the man who had been by Evelyn's side while Daniel had been at war, called this part of paradise home when he wasn't in town.

Cooper's friendship had become a steadying hand in the three months since Daniel's return. Without speaking of it, Cooper understood what Daniel had been through. They never spoke of their experiences: Daniel's in the war between the North and South, and Cooper's from his days serving as a civilian tracker in the army, occupying the West and witnessing the travesties wrought against the natives.

Cooper first brought Daniel to this same mountain lake a

week after the nightmares had begun. Since then, Daniel had found solace in this place high above the town, the people, the noise. When he craved silence, he came here. Daniel had seen the disappointment in Evelyn's eyes when he remained quiet about his experiences, but she never pushed.

He heard the crunch of horse hooves on rocks and twigs covering the trail. Only Cooper came here—it was his home. Daniel wondered where he had been for the past three days.

Daniel did turn when Cooper said nothing and saw the extra horse with the large buck draped over the saddle and covered in heavy canvas. Cooper walked over and stood next to Daniel. The dawn's warm sun promised a clear and sunny day.

"Thought you might be here this morning."

"The buck is for tonight?"

Cooper nodded. "Evelyn will understand if you aren't there."

"I can't do that to her." Daniel watched the sun inch higher on the horizon. The first Independence Day in four years without the screams, trumpets, cannons, and muskets echoing in his ears. Instead of a body-strewn battlefield, Daniel gazed upon the most beautiful valley he'd ever seen in his life. Instead of cries coming from a hospital tent, the town of Whitcomb Springs below was a haven for him and anyone else seeking solace and a peaceful place to live.

Daniel still heard the screams in his nightmares. Muskets firing, filling the air with the stench of smoke and death. He relived it often. Most nights, the comfort of holding his wife was enough to waylay the madness within, but the worst of the memories sneaked through his barrier.

"She doesn't ask about it."

Cooper said nothing for a few seconds, and then, "She may

not. Your wife never asked me about my days in the army, not once in four years."

"What about Abigail? Have you spoken with her about those years?" Daniel watched Cooper toss a pebble down the mountain.

Cooper nodded. "I couldn't court her without telling her everything. It wasn't easy. You've been back three months, and what you went through is nothing even I can imagine. Give it time."

"And did it help, telling Abigail?"

"Nothing has brought me more peace before or since."

Daniel kept his eyes focused on the rising sun. Soon it would be high enough to bring light to the entire valley. Where they sat, the mountain shielded them in its shadow. Turning to Cooper, he asked, "Do you ever regret not going?"

"Sometimes."

"I'm grateful you stayed, for what you did for Evelyn and this town." Daniel stood and walked back to his horse. It had remained close yet still wandered to find the sweetest grass with morning dew. "If I had known how long I would have been away—"

"No one knew how long it would last." Cooper also walked back to his horse, checking to make sure the large buck was still secure on the second animal. "And if our roles had been reversed, you would have done the same."

Daniel studied his friend. "Evelyn tells me you've been spending a lot of time with her sister."

Cooper grinned at him, and though Daniel reciprocated the smile, his heart remained heavy with too many memories. He lived in a constant fog with only glimpses of light, a brightness he found with Evelyn, but still the darkness remained beneath the surface, waiting to rise at unexpected times.

"Abigail is special. I love her, and I only tell you this so you know my intentions are honorable."

Daniel pulled himself into the saddle. "If I doubted that, I would have done something about you a long time ago." This time his sincere smile blew away some of the darker clouds as he headed down the mountain trail toward home.

THE TOWN WAS quiet as expected this time of morning, and yet an eerie silence filled the air like the mist still dispersed over the valley floor. He and Cooper traveled down from the mountain on a trail that connected to the north road leading into town. A hard-packed dirt road passed by Daniel and Evelyn's home, where Evelyn and Abigail could often be found in the garden at this early hour.

Evelyn doted on her flower gardens, but this morning the flowers stood alone, glistening with water droplets in the early morning light. The town's shared vegetable garden to the south of the house was also empty, tools set against the fence with no one to yield them.

"Mr. Whitcomb!" Cody Skeeters jumped up and down on the front porch of the big house and ran toward them. "Mrs. Whitcomb says I ain't supposed to move until you and Cooper get here!"

Daniel held up a hand and looked down at the boy. "Is she hurt?"

Cody shook his head. "There's a dead man, Mr. Whitcomb! A real dead man. I ain't never seen nothing like it."

"Come here, Cody." Cooper motioned the boy closer. "Where is he?"

Cody pointed toward town. "In the clearing next to Miss Maggie's saloon."

"You take this pack horse down to Mr. Andris at the blacksmith's barn. Can you do that for me?"

The boy nodded, his eyes still wide from excitement, and clasped the reins Cooper passed to him.

"Is Miss Abigail with her sister?"

Cody shook his head again. "I ain't seen Miss Abigail."

Both men urged their horses forward. Most of the townspeople had yet to leave their homes, which Daniel considered a blessing. His horse skidded to a halt a short distance from where a few early risers had gathered near the grass next to the saloon that also doubled as a restaurant, if one didn't need variety. The saloon didn't serve much beyond stew and biscuits or meatloaf, but it was one of the best meals in town.

He spotted Maggie Lynch, the proprietor, on the front boardwalk of the Blackwater Tavern, named after the pub her grandfather once operated in Ireland. Her wild, flame-red hair curled around her head and shoulders.

Daniel searched the faces but did not see his wife. His heart rate accelerated, as it always did when he thought of Evelyn in possible danger, and he pushed his way through the small circle of people.

He saw Evelyn kneeling on the ground next to a prone body covered with a canvas tarp. Daniel touched her shoulder, and when she looked at him, it was with damp and worried eyes. He helped his wife stand and took her place next to the body. Daniel inched the canvas away from the head, careful to block what he uncovered. Whitcomb Springs still awaited the new doctor, but the dead man did not need healing.

"What happened?"

No one immediately answered his question. Daniel heard Cooper move up beside him and ask, "Where's Abigail?"

"She's all right, Cooper. She went to the school early to prepare and doesn't know this has happened." Evelyn added, "Maggie found the body about a half hour ago. We wanted to move him, but then thought you and Daniel should see him first."

Daniel didn't yet know everyone in town, and from his appearance, he suspected the young man worked in the mine or timber camp. Cooper confirmed his suspicions.

"That's Jacob Smith. He was hired the start of this season at the mine." Cooper squatted and ran a hand along the back of Jacob's head to what appeared to be the source of the blood. "Feels like someone hit him. Had to have been a powerful blow to kill him."

Daniel looked up at his wife who now stood next to Maggie. He asked Maggie, "Did you or anyone else see what happened?"

Maggie shook her head. "I saw nothing. We don't open for hours so no one else was inside. I came outside to go walking, like I always do first thing, and saw Jacob instead."

"You know him?"

"Sure do," Maggie said. "He came into the saloon once a week for the meatloaf. Sweet kid, only nineteen years old."

"He dreamed of becoming a rancher," Evelyn said, another reminder at how much more Evelyn was connected to the town than he. Daniel helped wherever he could, went to church, frequented the businesses, but he realized he'd yet to allow himself to become a part of the town the way his wife had. He wasn't yet ready. A young man he never met—one of his employees—lay dead on the streets of his town. Daniel's days of mourning the years he'd lost to war were about to be over. Time to focus on the now.

The sun's path into the morning sky continued. Many who lived in town or nearby would soon appear. Men on the first shift at the timber camp would already be at work, and the mine would open for the day. Daniel shared a glance with Cooper, who nodded once and rose. Cooper pointed to two of them men standing nearby. "Help me carry him to the clinic."

One man felt it necessary to speak the obvious. "But there ain't no doc there."

"No, there isn't." Cooper motioned them over when Daniel moved out of the way. "But it's empty, close, and we have to get him off the street."

Daniel waited for them to carry the young man across the road before he faced his wife and Maggie. "You have an extra room over your saloon, is that right, Maggie?" He caught the look shared between the two women.

"I do."

"I'd feel better if your brother stayed with you until we find out what happened. I'm sure he wouldn't mind leaving the timber camp for a few days."

Maggie's eyes narrowed and Daniel looked to Evelyn for help. "Maggie, Daniel's right, it will only be for a short time, and it would ease my worry."

"Of all the—"

Cooper's return interrupted the start of Maggie's tirade.

"He has a point, Maggie. This happened in front of your

saloon. Might not be a coincidence."

"If I agree to this, I'm doing it for Evelyn." She pointed a finger at Cooper's chest.

"Understood, Maggie."

"We've got him! We've got the killer!" The shouts came from outside the circle of people, now parting to allow the newcomers passage to the center.

Daniel and Cooper watched a tall, black man being dragged toward them by two miners Daniel had met soon after his return home. Daniel stared in shock. Before him, hands bound and blood on his shirt stood Gordon Wells, the former slave who had saved his life.

DANIEL REACHED FOR Gordon's bound hands and pulled him away from the men who had brought him forward. "This man is not a killer." Daniel untied Gordon's hands and said to the crowd, "Unless you have definitive proof that this man has done anything wrong, he'll be released until we can investigate.

One of the would-be captors said while pointing at Gordon, "We have no sheriff, and I know what's right in front of me. He's got blood on his shirt."

Daniel knew most of the residents were still getting used to him. Evelyn had been the matriarch of Whitcomb Springs for four years, and many of the people now living and working for them had only ever heard of the man who went off to fight in the war. Daniel remembered the accuser's name—Abraham—but nothing else about him.

Cooper eased the man back a few paces from Daniel and Gordon. "Do you trust me, Abraham?"

Abraham pulled his gaze away and glanced at Cooper. "I do. You saved me when my leg got caught under a beam in the mine."

"Then trust me to investigate what happened here. If Daniel knows and trusts this man, that should be good enough for all of us."

Abraham faced Daniel again, this time with wariness visible in his eyes, before he walked away.

"Daniel?"

He held out a hand for his wife. "Evelyn, I'd like you to meet Gordon Wells."

Daniel watched moisture gather in Evelyn's eyes. Without hesitation, she embraced the man's hands. "Thank you for saving my husband's life."

"I feared somethin' bad when dey found me. I sure am glad you is here, Mr. Whitcomb."

Cooper handled the few people who had remained to watch the drama unfold and told them to go about their own business. They had a town supper to get ready for that evening. Daniel and Evelyn had celebrated their country's day of independence every year when they'd been at home. When they ventured west, they'd had only one year of peace before Daniel left, and the celebrating ceased. Most of the people dispersed, casting curious glances toward the Whitcombs and the newcomer, but neither Daniel or Evelyn paid them any mind.

"You used to call me Daniel. I hope you'll do so again." He looked to Maggie and asked, "May we use your saloon for a few minutes?"

"Of course. You go right on in and I'll make sure no one disturbs you. Lord sake's, I never imagined something like this happening here." Maggie shook her head and ushered them inside, closing the double doors behind them.

Evelyn rushed behind the long, polished bar and returned with a glass of water for Gordon. "Please, sit and rest."

Eyes wide and hesitant, Gordon circled his large hand around the glass and gulped down half the contents. "I thank you, ma'am."

Daniel remained standing next Gordon, waited a few minutes for his old friend to regain his bearings.

"I done caused you folks trouble."

"No, you haven't." Daniel pulled a chair out for his wife before he moved one so he could sit and face Gordon. "Tell me what's happened. The blood on your shirt is drying, but still fresh. You've got a cut on your lip, but I know it didn't come from killing anyone. No one who goes to the trouble of saving a person would take a life without good reason."

"I was huntin' for my family. We is camped maybe two miles from here."

"You were coming to Whitcomb Springs?"

Gordon glanced briefly at Evelyn. "Yes, ma'am. I remember Mr.—Daniel here sayin' how if I wanted, I ought to come. There weren't nothin' else for our family where we was, so here we is."

"I meant it, and I hoped you would find your way here." Daniel glanced toward the door as new shouting ensued. "We need to see that your family is brought safely to town. Your wife and daughter, correct?"

Gordon nodded. "Dey is waiting for me. I walked more'n I thought following the deer."

"Where did they find you?"

"I realized how close I came to town and thought to borrow

a horse from de blacksmith. Dat's when dem two men found me. The blood is from the deer I left in de woods."

"I believe you, Gordon." Daniel's eyes met his wife's, and an unspoken understanding passed between them. "Your family won't understand if someone shows up in your stead. We'll leave out the back and go to them together. My horse is out front, but we need our wagon."

Evelyn said, "I'll take your horse back to the house."

Daniel looked over his shoulder and through the windows at the front of the saloon. A larger crowd now gathered, curious about the red-stained grass. None of them looked inside but rather to where the body had lain. That would soon change. Daniel knew most folks in town cared more about truth and kindness than speculation, but a few wouldn't be generous to Gordon's presence after losing some of their own in a fight believed by some to solely be about ending slavery. It wasn't Gordon's fault, yet fear and bigotry too often clouded initial reactions. For some, their judgment began and ended with ignorance.

"Leave the horse. I'll saddle another when we get to the barn."

Evelyn nodded and pointed toward the back door. "I'll wait a few seconds before going out front with Maggie."

"Tell Cooper where we've gone, just in case we are not back in two hours. It shouldn't take longer than that to get there and return." Daniel squeezed his wife's hand and led Gordon out the rear door. He glanced back once at Evelyn before making sure the area was clear. The short line of businesses on the one main road in town backed up to the Whitcomb's land, only part of it treed. They didn't have to worry about coming across anyone else, but someone might still see them crossing behind the community garden to the barn.

Daniel prayed everyone remained distracted enough as they ran, hunched over, toward the barn.

EVELYN STEPPED ONTO the front porch of the saloon as quietly as possible, closing the door behind her. She nodded once to Cooper, who stood nearby answering questions as they were asked from the few who remained behind. Most people had left as told, but Evelyn wanted no one else around when she informed Cooper where Daniel and Gordon had gone.

A few folks came and went. Others who had recently awakened or ventured into town stopped out of curiosity. News of a dead man, especially one many of them knew, spread quicker than a wildfire on the prairie. No one paid much attention to Evelyn or Maggie, but Evelyn knew it wouldn't be long before someone noticed and wondered what the women were doing.

Evelyn leaned closer to Maggie. "I need to find Abigail, tell her what's happened. This won't be contained long, and soon there will be speculation about Gordon's whereabouts. We need to give him and Daniel time to return with Gordon's family."

Maggie perused the crowd and waved to a pair of women Evelyn recognized as new in town with their miner husbands. Maggie said, "You find your sister. How long does Daniel need?"

"He said two hours."

Maggie nodded. "I'll handle things here with Cooper, deflect inquiries for as long as possible."

Evelyn laid a hand on Maggie's arm in a gentle gesture of appreciation. "Thank you, Maggie. This man accused of murder, he saved Daniel's life. I cannot allow anyone—"

Maggie covered Evelyn's hand and squeezed. "I understand. If that boy was killed, and we don't know for certain he was, I'd rather believe no one would do such a thing. Go now, but slowly so as not to draw attention."

By way of distraction, Maggie walked the length of the saloon porch until she perched on the top step that led down to the grassy area where the body had been discovered. She drew any curious onlookers' gazes to her, giving Evelyn time to make her way to the school.

Evelyn did not cross paths with anyone on her way to the meadow where the school was situated near a brook. The serenity of the setting belied the morning's events. What began as a peaceful day, a day of celebration for their country, turned into a tragedy. Evelyn had prayed for calm and peace for Daniel's sake.

He'd blessedly spent the previous evening free of nightmares, but she longed for a time when weeks or months would pass without the terrors of war revisiting him in slumber. He did not speak of their years apart in detail and she did not ask. She soothed him while he slept, allowing him to return to sleep without knowing his own anguish. Other nights, they awoke together, Daniel dripping with sweat and Evelyn trying to ease her racing heart. On those nights, Daniel left their bed to stand outside in the cool, night air, returning only when his breathing had calmed.

Evelyn picked up her pace as she approached the schoolhouse, shaking the thoughts of hopelessness away. Abigail sat at the scarred-top desk at the front of the small room when Evelyn pushed in through the double door.

They knew each other so well, Evelyn and her sister. Abigail immediately stood and hurried to meet Evelyn halfway.

"What's happened?"

Evelyn tried to ease the worry lines from her face, but from the expression her sister wore, she'd been unsuccessful. "Jacob Smith, a young miner, died sometime this morning in the clearing next to Maggie's saloon."

Abigail squeezed her sister's hands. "I knew Jacob. He came to me only yesterday to ask if I could teach him how to read." Abigail's chest heaved with heavy breaths.

Evelyn eased her into one of the student's seats. "There's more, I'm afraid. Do you remember Daniel mentioned a man named Gordon Wells?"

Abigail nodded. "The slave who saved him near the end of the war."

"That's right. Daniel told Gordon to come to Whitcomb Springs should he ever wish to start anew. Well, Gordon has arrived, and one of the miners dragged him into town this morning."

"And he's suspected in the murder."

Evelyn raised a brow at her sister. "How did you guess?"

"I heard stories during the war about the mistreatment of slaves. How even those who did nothing wrong were considered criminals. People do not change so quickly, nor do they forget." Abigail stood now on steadier legs. "Gordon has unfortunate timing."

"Yes, although I believe he decided to come here when Daniel first offered."

"Then he's been traveling for some time. Does he have family with him?" Abigail asked.

"He does, a wife and daughter. They'll be staying with us for now."

Evelyn watched her sister's expression of understanding turn to one of disbelief.

Abigail said, "By the way you're looking at me, you seem to believe that will bother me. You forget, Evie, I was closer to the conflicts. Still protected, yes, but I witnessed men and women being smuggled into the North. No one should have to live with so much fear."

Evelyn blinked a few times. "You said nothing. To be close enough to see, you would have been helping . . . Oh, dear. I assume no one knew."

"Yes, I assisted at a stop on the Underground Railroad. I brought food and other supplies to help those newly arrived. For our family's sake, I kept some distance, but I would not be stopped from helping."

Evelyn blinked again, this time to keep tears of both belated worry and pride from escaping. She cleared her throat and composed herself before saying, "Part of why I came to tell you is so you're not surprised if parents keep their children from class today when they hear of what's happened. Some of them will hesitate to let the young ones wander far from their sides. We will need your help to calm the ripple effects of conjecture."

"Should I close the school for a few days?"

Evelyn glanced at the silver watch fob attached to her apron, the apron she still wore when she was interrupted in the garden earlier. She considered both the benefits and the consequences of keeping the children away and shook her head. "Parents who live outside town will not hear of Jacob's death before school begins. Many of their children walk to town alone and it is better that they have a place to go."

"Of course. Please let me know when Daniel returns."

"I will."

"And Evie?"

Evelyn turned back to face her sister.

"Was anyone else injured?"

Evelyn understood the unspoken question. "Cooper returned with Daniel this morning. He is safe."

DANIEL AND GORDON reached the Wells's camp by way of the main road. Travelers rarely journeyed to and from Whitcomb Springs since the stage did not yet stop in their valley, but as word of the timber and mining jobs spread throughout the territory, men and families came in search of work.

Someday the stage, and perhaps a spur line, would benefit their small town, but today, Daniel was grateful they lived at the end of a less traveled road. Daniel noticed the smoke from a campfire before Gordon indicated they'd arrived. The camp was not visible from the road, but Gordon whistled twice and half a minute later a woman and child emerged from the trees.

They smiled when Gordon climbed down from the buckboard's seat, but gave pause when they noticed Daniel atop his horse. He remained in the saddle until after Gordon embraced them and explained Daniel's presence. Gordon's wife, Hany Wells, took a few tentative steps toward Daniel's horse. After almost of minute of studying him, she waved him down to join them.

Daniel witnessed what the slaves had suffered at the hands of their masters, yet he still could not imagine the depths of their fear when confronted by a white man. He did not fool himself into believing their journey to Montana had been without great difficulty and unease.

Hany was a handsome woman with round, brown eyes, wide smile, and a complexion one shade lighter than her husband's. She wore her dark, loosely curled hair at her nape, and took pains to straighten her frayed apron. Their daughter was as becoming as her mother.

Daniel approached the family out of respect and surprised them all. "It is indeed a pleasure to meet you, Mrs. Wells."

When Hany smiled, Daniel believed it was with sincerity. "It's nice to meet you, Mr. Whitcomb. This here is our girl, Grace. Gordon's done talked about you all de way here. But how is you here, Mr. Whitcomb?"

"Please, call me Daniel." He looked to Gordon before responding to the question. "There's been trouble in town. Nothing to alarm you," he assured her, "but it is best if we return. Is your camp easy to pack up?"

Hany nodded, but Daniel did not miss the concerned glance she cast toward her husband. "Is you in trouble, Gordon?"

"I reckon maybe so, Hany, but Mr.—Daniel—say I's not to worry. We is close now, Hany. We is real close."

Hany's doubt showed on her face when she looked at Daniel. "Is that de truth?"

"I promise, you will all be safe. I will explain on the way, but let us hurry now."

EVELYN TENDED TO her flowers, though her heart was not in the work. She pulled a weed and then an herb, not noticing the difference until the healthy plant hung from her fingers, dirt crumbling back to earth. Evelyn replanted the herb, taking care to cover the roots again.

She looked up every time she heard someone on the road, each time reminding herself they would not come through town, yet she continued to look and hope. Two hours had come and gone, and still the day had not yet shifted from morning.

Cooper and two men he'd chosen were watching over the body. Poor Jacob Smith would need to be prepared for burial. The nights brought cooler air but the days burned warm, and they could not leave him aboveground for more than a day or two.

After her visit with Abigail, she'd spent an hour assuring families who inquired that there was no danger to anyone, only she wished the words held more conviction. They did not know who killed one of their own or why. She hoped everyone would follow Maggie's lead and believe no one among them could kill another. Jacob was a young man and hard worker. He would not have had much on him except his weekly earnings, distributed the day before to all of the miners. The men working timber and building the new sawmill would receive their pay today, which led Evelyn to doubt one of their workers had done this.

"Evelyn?"

She glanced up and saw the mine foreman's wife approach the fence. "Mrs. Cosgrove."

"Is it true what I've just heard, Evelyn?"

"Yes, Lillian, I'm afraid it is."

"In our town, a murderer is running loose. It's not to be borne, Evelyn."

Lillian Cosgrove preferred city life to the small mountain

valley, but this was where her husband had come so it's where she lived.

"Oh, Lillian, there is not a killer loose among us, and I do not believe anyone else is in danger. Cooper and Daniel will discover what happened, and in the meantime, is our energy not better spent on prayers for the departed?"

"Well, of course, but—"

"And should we not be mindful of the town's children, assuring them that there is nothing to fear? Your own daughter will want to know you are not concerned, is that not true?"

"Yes, it is, but we need a proper sheriff."

Evelyn used the trowel to help stand from the flower bed. She gave her apron a cursory dusting. "We have a proper sheriff. Mr. Jenkins has accepted the position and will arrive any day now."

"But it has been more than a month since he accepted. Surely someone else is interested in the position."

"We received other replies, but none as qualified as Abbott Jenkins. He's leaving the Pinkertons to come here. We want to be sure we have the best for our town, for the people. Do you not agree?"

Lillian's bodice swelled when she stood straighter and inhaled deeply. Her chin rose a fraction higher than necessary. "I do agree."

"The committee to hire a new schoolteacher could do with another member."

The other woman's demeanor shifted in quick degrees. Evelyn knew many of the townspeople's idiosyncrasies and weaknesses, and Lillian's weakness was her desire for recognition and control. She meant well, and Evelyn had learned to handle

Lillian, and the few others like her, with care.

"Are you asking me?"

Lillian knew what Evelyn meant, but Evelyn still acknowledged her with a nod. "We would be pleased to have you on the committee."

"Then it would be my honor."

Evelyn hid a smile. "It won't be easy finding someone to fill the post, so you must be patient."

"I will be ready." Lillian pressed a hand to her corset-held middle and fluttered away in better spirits than when she'd arrived. Evelyn believed the good mood would last only a few minutes, until Lillian remembered why she had visited Evelyn in the first place.

Evelyn heard what she'd been waiting for and was slow to move, waving to Lillian when she glanced over her shoulder. When no one else was around, Evelyn picked up her tools and carried them to the shed near the edge of the garden. In her peripheral, she observed movement and recognized Daniel's tall frame. The others were a blur when they hurried into the barn.

The buckboard remained outside, and a minute later Daniel reemerged to take care of the wagon and horses. Evelyn said his name when she was still a dozen feet away, so as not to startle him, but he must have already sensed her presence for he turned toward her.

"They are safe?"

He nodded and brought her into his arms. "They are. Frightened, but doing well considering."

"Did Gordon tell her what happened?"

"Some of it, but not all because of their daughter. Her name is Grace. She's a sweet girl."

Evelyn heard the wistfulness in her husband's voice. "We'll have one of our own someday. We can fill the house with laughter and love."

Daniel smoothed a hand over his gelding's flank and removed the saddle. "Someday."

Evelyn reminded herself that he wanted children as much as she did, but fear continued to grip him, fear of his own mortality, and fear that the scars he carried home with him would pass onto their son or daughter. They had tried and failed in the past. She held her counsel and leaned up to press a kiss to his cheek. "I'll prepare food for them. It's safe to bring them into the house now. "

"Is Harriet here?"

Evelyn shook her head in question to the young widow who often worked at the Whitcomb's house to help with the housekeeping and gardens. "She's helping Abigail at the school today, and I'll let her and Tabitha know they won't be needed around here the remainder of the week. I preferred not to have anyone around before you came back, and I don't want our guests to be uncomfortable. I informed Abigail that Gordon and his family would stay here for a few days." Evelyn noticed now only one additional horse, a tired creature who deserved a permanent home in a grassy pasture. "Did they travel all this way with only the one animal?"

"They did. Gordon walked most of the way."

"And so far." Evelyn brushed a tear as soon as it fell on her cheek. "I won't be long. We need not wait until darkness comes to bring them inside. I've been watching, and there is no one about. Those who are in town are more curious about what happened to Jacob."

"Then word hasn't gotten out about Gordon?"

"I have not heard talk of it. The miner who first accused Gordon should be working. Cooper is at the clinic; I told him where you'd gone."

Evelyn kept a brisk pace on her walk back to the house and felt Daniel's eyes on her the entire way. She stopped and walked past her husband to the barn. When she entered, the three inhabitants moved deeper into a corner until Gordon recognized Evelyn.

"Hello, Mrs. Whitcomb."

"Please, Gordon, it's Evelyn."

"Yes, ma'am. This here is my missus, Hany, and our girl, Grace."

Evelyn held her hand out to Gordon's wife, and only after gentle prodding from her husband did Hany accept the gesture of friendship. "It is my honor to meet you, Mrs. Wells, and your beautiful daughter. Your husband saved my life, too, when he saved Mr. Whitcomb."

"De good Lord was watchin' over them both dat day."

"Yes, He was. Now, I've prepared rooms in the house for you. If Grace prefers not to have her own room right now, then Daniel can bring a cot into your bedroom. We'll get you settled into a place of your own soon. For a few days, I hope you will consent to be our guests."

Both Gordon and Hany looked flabbergasted. Gordon said, "We is fine in de barn."

"I won't hear of it."

"She never loses an argument, Gordon," Daniel said from behind Evelyn.

Gordon merely nodded and whispered something for only his

wife to hear. Their daughter Grace, who appeared six or seven, tugged on her mother's arm, and said in a barely perceptible voice, "Are we home now, Mama?"

Hany raised cautious and hopeful eyes to Evelyn and Daniel. "I suspect we is, Gracie girl."

"WE'LL NEED TO cancel the celebration tonight."

Daniel watched his wife prepare tea. Her quick hands and long fingers didn't waste a movement. They were alone in the kitchen while the Wells family rested upstairs in the guest rooms. Young Grace had preferred to stay with her parents, until she saw the big bed that was offered to her. She had approached the bed with shy wonder, running her hand over the colorful quilt Evelyn had made her second winter in Montana. It proved to be a pleasant and useful hobby that helped pass the time during the long, cold months. Daniel recalled his surprise upon seeing that quilt, and three others, when he arrived, and even more surprise when Evelyn confessed she'd made them. Her skills had always been more academic and in managing a household, rather than in domestic pursuits.

Cooper had sent a note by way of young Cody Skeeters that they would prepare the ground for Jacob's burial.

Daniel returned his thoughts to her comment and offered one of his own. "I'm not certain we should cancel."

Evelyn set the teapot on the linen-covered table and stared at him. "Jacob Smith will need to be buried tomorrow. How can we celebrate anything with what's happened?"

Jacob's was not the first suspect death Daniel had ever witnessed. Desperate men committed abominable crimes, and in the past four years, Daniel had seen too many desperate men. When the only stories he carried with him were of death and destruction, it was impossible to share those missing years with Evelyn.

"We make it a celebration of Jacob's life, of his dreams. We celebrate in his honor and in the town's future."

"It is a wonderful idea, but I feel that is not your only purpose."

"No, it's not." Daniel accepted the cup of fragrant tea. "I need to be certain no one else comes looking for Gordon. He did not do this, and I promised his family he would be safe. I expect just about everyone who lives and works in Whitcomb Springs to attend. Whoever isn't . . . Well, that will be telling."

"You're going to meet Cooper."

Evelyn always seemed to know Daniel's thoughts and plans before he did. "I am. I won't be long, but I need to see this through. It is time for me to look after this town, the way you and Cooper have."

"You do, Daniel."

"Not in the way I should. I labor and we give money where needed to help the town grow, but I have not allowed myself to become a part of this place, these people, not like when we first arrived." Daniel drank a bit of the tea to placate Evelyn. When he pushed back his chair and stood, he eased her into his embrace. "I promise you, I will no longer be a ghost."

Without waiting for a reply, he pressed his lips to hers, allowing himself to savor and memorize everything her nearness made him feel, and he left.

DANIEL ENTERED THE clinic and closed the door behind him. Cooper nodded once to Daniel before returning his attention to Jacob. A fresh canvas had been placed over the body, and only his head and arm were uncovered.

The building boasted a generous front room, a back office, and like most businesses in town, comfortable living quarters on the second floor. They had equipped the clinic with all the basic accoutrements of a doctor's office, and planned to leave the remaining details to the physician, when they found one.

"How is Gordon and his family?"

"They're resting and understandably worried. When I was still in nursery school, my father spoke of slavery in the South and explained that no man had the right to own another. I remember agreeing with him, but I never—never—understood what any of it meant until I met Gordon. Even those first few years of war, I was still in the North. When Gordon saved me, knowing the consequences, he taught me more about freedom and fairness than I'd learned at any point in my life." Daniel had been staring at the body laid out on the long table in the center of the office. He had not meant to say so much and was grateful when Cooper kept silent. "Have you found anything?"

Cooper motioned Daniel over. "It sure would be easier if a doctor was here to look him over, but there's no mistaking this." Cooper raised Jacob's arm and pushed up the sleeve. Daniel studied the unmistakable double punctures of a snake bite. The arm had swelled around the bite.

"Rattlesnake."

"That's what it looks like. We rarely spot a prairie rattler up here, and we've never had someone in town bit by one. I've seen this before, though." Colton lowered Jacob's arm. "I checked the bump on the back of his head again. It could have happened from a hard fall off his horse. If he was bit, he might not have been able to stay in the saddle."

"You think it's possible he was bit, got on his horse to come into town, and fell."

"Better explanation than someone we know maybe killed him. We'd have to find his horse to confirm the theory."

Daniel felt the back of Jacob's head. "Have you looked around again where he was found?"

"Yes, but I'm not sure it helps too much. There are few rocks there, one with blood that could have killed him when he landed. I relieved two men from the mine today to stand by and make sure no one disturbed the area. Folks have mostly moved on now. A lot of them are still asking questions. I've let it get around that this was an accident. Hope I'm right."

"So do I." Daniel raised the canvas over Jacob's face. "Whether or not he fell, he would have died from the bite. There's no one around here with medical knowledge enough to have saved him from the venom."

"I've treated a few snake bites, though his arm looks like he was too far gone already." Cooper walked around the body toward the door. "We need to find Jacob's horse. It should have stayed close."

Daniel stepped outside with Cooper. Someone had positioned two more men at either end of the wide porch in front of the clinic. Daniel acknowledged both and said to Cooper, "That no one has seen or found the horse yet is worrying. Stolen, perhaps?"

"I'm thinking so. Jacob bought his horse from Dominik Andris last week."

"Do you remember what the horse looks like?"

Cooper nodded. "If he's wandering loose, we'll find him."

"It's more likely the horse was taken." Daniel rubbed a hand over the back of his neck and looked toward the mountains. "I don't believe there's a killer amongst us, but theft is another matter. We've hired on a few new people the past month, still strangers. If we don't locate the animal, our next step will be to see who of the men have left unexpectedly."

When Cooper didn't answer, Daniel glanced his way and followed the direction of his attention—the school. "Have you spoken with Abigail yet today?"

"It was the first thing I had planned to do this morning, and then this happened."

"Go and see her. Harriett is helping at the school, so Abigail can step away for a few minutes."

Cooper murmured an affirmation of Daniel's suggestion, yet made no move to leave. Daniel considered his friend and confidant carefully, recognizing Cooper's indecision for what it truly was. Daniel said, "You had other plans for tonight, important plans, didn't you?"

"I did."

"I spoke with Evelyn earlier, and it seems to me that tonight's celebration should move forward. If we can assure everyone that Jacob's death was an accident, we can celebrate the day in honor of him, of all the men who have been lost. Jacob was young and eager and a soldier deserving of a nobler way to leave this life. I don't want another year passing without us having reason to celebrate our independence. It's important."

He anticipated Cooper's surprise. Daniel explained, "Evelyn told me that Jacob fought for the Confederacy."

"Does it bother you, knowing he was on the other side?"

"It might have, in the beginning. It wasn't long into the war when I realized that most men on both sides didn't want to be there. We kept going, fighting, killing . . ." Daniel shook the memory of the last battle from his thoughts. "No, it doesn't matter." He slapped Cooper on the shoulder, a friendly and masculine gesture meant to show affection. It was the only closeness Daniel could get to people these days—everyone except Evelyn. "I'll see if anyone didn't show up for their shift at the mine or timber camp." This time he offered his friend a smile. "Make sure you go and see Abigail before you look for Jacob's horse. And Cooper, you should ask her to step outside. You still smell like three days on the trail."

AS EVELYN STEPPED away from the clinic, she saw Cooper walking toward the schoolhouse. He had a lead on her but she was saved from an undignified shout when a woman stopped him. When Evelyn closed the distance between them, she called his name.

Cooper and the woman—Nettie Sandstrom, a newcomer to town with her husband—turned toward her. "Evelyn."

Evelyn smiled at Nettie and offered her hand. Though her errand was one of urgency, her position to help maintain calm was paramount. "How are you and your husband settling in, Nettie?"

"Oh, we're settling in just fine, Mrs. Whitcomb. The welcome basket you brought over was the nicest thing, and everyone here has been so kind. I was convinced Taylor had plumb lost his mind when he told me about this place. I was happy in Salt Lake

City, but I'm glad he convinced me to come."

Evelyn retrieved her hand from Nettie's enthusiastic grip and kept her smile trained on the young woman. Nineteen-year-old Nettie and twenty-year-old Taylor Sandstrom reminded Evelyn of her and Daniel when they first dreamed of what their future might hold. "Whitcomb Springs is lucky to have you."

Nettie's smile wavered, her glance darting from Evelyn to Cooper and back again. "Mr. McCord says there's no cause to worry over what happened with that poor miner this morning."

"Mr. McCord is right, and please let everyone you come across know we will still have our Independence Day celebration in the meadow this evening."

Nettie bobbed her head, made her excuses, and said goodbye. Evelyn watched her leave and noticed Nettie now walked with a lighter step. To Cooper she said, "I've always found telling one or two women any news in town ensures it will reach everyone. Nettie has already proven to have a fondness for socializing."

Cooper's mouth lifted up at the edges. "You mean gossip."

"Socializing sounds better."

"Uh-huh. What's wrong? You looked fierce walking toward us before."

"You saw me?"

Cooper nodded. "Briefly before Mrs. Sandstrom demanded my full attention."

Evelyn walked toward the schoolhouse. "You must be on your way to see Abigail. I was looking for Daniel and then I saw you coming here. I hoped you knew where he had gone."

"To the mine. He rode out a few minutes ago, but I can bring him back." Cooper relayed to her what he and Daniel had discussed and their conclusion that Jacob's death was likely the result of a snake bite and unfortunate fall. He explained Daniel's mission to the mine to see if anyone had decided to not show up for work, perhaps having left with a new horse.

"That is a tremendous relief. I am sorry for young Jacob, but the thought of someone we know—"

"Those were our sentiments, too. Now, what brought you out here looking for Daniel?"

"Gordon is missing."

Cooper stopped, forcing Evelyn to stop, too, or walk into him. "When?"

"I don't know exactly. I was in the kitchen, he must have left by the back door. I took a tray of food upstairs so they could eat and continue resting. Hany and Grace were still asleep and neither heard him leave." Evelyn moved her eyes over the school's white-washed front door when it opened. Abigail stepped outside and waved. "I would go for Daniel myself—"

"I'll be able to catch him before he reaches the mine. Please explain to Abigail for me and tell her . . . tell her I won't be long."

Cooper moved quickly on his feet, reaching his horse by the time Abigail stepped alongside Evelyn and looped her arm through hers.

"Where is he off to in such a rush?"

"To fetch Daniel."

Evelyn subjected herself to Abigail's scrutiny when her sister forced her to turn. "Is everything all right?"

"I'm not sure." Evelyn patted her sister's hand so she would ease her grasp. "It will be, I know that much. Cooper won't be long. I would not have asked him to go if it wasn't important. He has been anxious to see you since this morning."

Abigail's rose-tinged cheeks darkened with her blush. "I have been eager to see him, too. I am used to his hunting excursions, but it is becoming more difficult to be apart from . . ." Abigail's blush lightened when her words faltered. "I'm so sorry, Evie. You know more than anyone what it is like, and here I am complaining of a few days."

"There is no need to worry or apologize, Abigail. I've had Daniel back home and in my arms for almost three months now. Soon those four years will be a faded memory." Evelyn doubted the truth of her words the second she thought them, though they brought comfort to say them aloud.

"Will you tell me what's wrong, Evie?"

Distracted by the comings and goings of people, Evelyn murmured an affirmative to her sister. Her focus, however, remained on the front of her house. From where she stood in the meadow with Abigail, she could see part of gardens, the porch, and the rise of the barn behind the house. If she moved a few feet to the left, the mercantile would block her view. As it happened, she glimpsed enough to make her curious. "I must go. I promise to explain everything soon, but I need to check on someone."

"Evie." Abigail held fast to her arm. "Did someone kill Jacob or was it an accident? Harriet believes someone murdered him and heard as much from someone—she failed to mention who—before she arrived at the school."

"Harriett's information has gaps." Evelyn shouldn't have been surprised, and yet sometimes the network of news through town marveled even her. She did not want to speculate on who took the trouble to rush to tell Harriett of the goings-on. Evelyn recalled the reassuring words Cooper gave her. "After further investigation, it's believed it was a tragic accident. There is no reason for anyone to worry anymore. I promise, all will be well. School is letting out early today, yes?"

Abigail nodded. "The children are making decorations and practicing lines for the songs they plan to sing tonight. Harriett said the celebration will continue."

"How she heard already is baffling. Yes, our plans have not changed. Well, not entirely. Don't be late tonight."

With those parting words, Evelyn left her sister to hurry home. Haste was not easily achieved when people stopped her progression. She rushed through assurances the best she could but quickly disengaged herself from each conversation. When she arrived at the house, she stopped on the porch, her hand ready to open the front door. The sobbing on the other side of the door, or more precisely, through one of the open windows in her sitting room, gave Evelyn pause. It was the unexpected voice that prompted her expedited entry into the house.

She found Gordon holding his wife and daughter in his wide embrace. They were slight enough for his arms to encircle them both and hold them close. Gordon's eyes met hers when she stepped into the room.

"I's sorry, Mrs. Whitcomb. Hany done told me I scared de life out of her."

Evelyn's pounding heart slowed with each step closer to the family. She stopped five feet away, not wanting to encroach. She would have preferred to leave them alone entirely, only it was imperative she speak with Gordon.

"Daniel should be here soon." Evelyn cast a furtive glance to Grace before asking, "Where did you go, Gordon, and why did you not say anything?"

"I can explain."

Evelyn realized her mistake. "I am not upset, but like your family, I worried for your safety. Cooper told me that he and Daniel believe they can prove the young man this morning died by an accident, but until they can find the men who accused you, and explain what happened, you are safer here."

Gordon leaned his head low to his wife's ear and whispered, meant only for her. Hany nodded, gathered Grace in her arms, and urged the young girl from the room. When they had left, Gordon faced Evelyn with all the contrition of a man on his way to the gallows.

"You got a right to be angry, Mrs. Whitcomb. Hany sure is."

Evelyn felt her mouth twitch. "Hany was worried, too."

"I should've told you. Hany lost her locket. I saw it missing and it was her mama's. Didn't seem right to leave it out in dem woods."

A deep breath filled Evelyn's lungs, and when she released it, the tension in her body went with it. "That was thoughtful of you, Gordon. I'm sure Hany appreciated your effort in retrieving such a precious item. Did you find it?"

Gordon nodded. "I figured where she might of lost it. She stumbled gettin' out of de wagon. I figure I'd be back inside 'afore anyone noticed."

They both looked to the open, front door when they heard the pounding of hooves on the hard-packed dirt road. Only one rider, Evelyn surmised, and as though she had memorized the sound of Daniel's unique step, she knew it was him before she glanced out the window.

DANIEL HALTED ONCE inside and examined the scene

before him. Gordon appeared guilty and Evelyn's face expressed relief. Cooper had known only what Evelyn told him, that Gordon was missing.

"I feared the worst, friend." Daniel held out his hand and waited for Gordon to accept it. They stepped back again. "It is your business if you come and go, and not ours, but with your wife and child left behind, you must have known everyone would worry about you."

Evelyn linked her arm with his, drawing some of his frustration away. "It is all right, Daniel. Gordon explained that he left only to search for Hany's locket. She lost it somewhere when exiting the wagon. The mistake was mine, in fearing he had gone, when he was just near the barn. If I had not alerted Hany and Grace that he was not here, they likely would have remained asleep."

"I should've said somethin', Mrs. Whitcomb."

Daniel listened to his wife's self-recrimination and Daniel's apology. He understood why Gordon went on his errand without telling anyone, just as he understood Evelyn's concern when Gordon was not where she thought he should be.

Daniel whispered to his wife, "I need to speak with Gordon, for only a few minutes." He looked at his friend. "Would you walk with me outside? We won't be long."

Gordon nodded and followed Daniel out the front door. Daniel waited until Gordon fell into step beside him when his instinct would have been to walk behind. They walked the trail leading toward the creek before Daniel spoke. "A week after I came home, Evelyn came to our room expecting to find me. She insisted I rest and was bringing me a tray of food. What she found was an empty bed and room. I had left the house without telling her, much like you did. I was not accustomed to explaining myself to anyone except my commanding officer. Unfortunately, I saw the effect of my blunder when I returned two hours later from a walk. Since then, I make sure to tell her where I am or where I will be going."

He stopped by the creek and for a few seconds remained silent so only the sound of the water smoothing over rocks filled the air. "Evelyn's reaction was more likely an echo of what she felt that day, and nothing you did wrong. I explain this only because I know why you said nothing to her when you went outside. You were born into slavery, and not a moment of your life has gone by when you didn't have to account for it. You've earned your freedom, Gordon. Do not feel guilty for using it. Please, we only hope you will be careful until the matter with Jacob Smith is resolved. It won't take much longer for everyone to hear that you are not to blame."

Gordon stared, not saying a single word for two minutes. "Hany says I still gots to say sorry again to Mrs. Whitcomb. If Hany wants somethin'—"

"Hany will get it." Daniel's chuckle mingled with the sound of lapping water. "Come, friend. Let us return. I still have a task to see to."

"I wants to help, if I can."

"Stay at the house and keep the women happy knowing they won't have any more worries today. You would be helping a lot."

Gordon grinned. "Ain't dat de truth."

DANIEL KISSED HIS wife. Hard and fast. He swung onto the back of his horse and returned to the mine to complete his earlier errand. The morning had moved into afternoon, and under the brighter sun, people set up makeshift tables in the meadow. Word had spread that the celebration would continue, which meant Cooper had told someone that Jacob's death was an accident. All it took was telling one person.

Accidents happened daily in the wilderness. They did all right without a town doctor, but people still died from injuries and illness. What happened to Jacob was unfortunate and made worse that he died on their day of independence. One could look upon it as Jacob's liberation from this life into a better one. Daniel had lost friends in battle and found some comfort believing they passed on to a more desirable place, free of pestilence, hunger, and eventual death. He was grateful Fate had spared him, and he owed his existence to sheer luck and Evelyn.

He arrived at the mine and slowed his horse to a meander and finally stopped him at a rise before the road eased down. The placer gold mine had not been boom-to-bust as expected. The gold was separated from the topsoil by running it through sluices, leaving the heavier gold pieces to sink while the dirt and lighter particles washed away with the water. They had been successful for a year before deciding they needed to find an alternative method for when the gold was no longer easy to find.

When Cooper first showed Daniel the mine and explained how they began digging and hauling, Daniel marveled at what had been accomplished during his time away. His inheritance had bought the land and built the town, but it was the hard work and ingenuity of the people that allowed it to prosper.

He had only one condition on continuing the mine—that the landscape would not be destroyed. If the time came when tunneling became too dangerous, they would close the mine rather than resort to hydraulic mining. Daniel had seen the effects of it on the environment and refused to destroy their land in such a manner.

Studying the operation below him, Daniel silently thanked Evelyn and Cooper for agreeing with him. When the mine eventually closed down, as was the natural order of mines, they would work to restore to the land close to its former beauty.

The foreman, Jedediah Cosgrove, waved Daniel down when he spotted him on the rise. They had made Jedediah foreman two months prior when the previous foreman decided he had suffered enough from Montana winters. He was bound for Arizona one week later and they offered Jedediah the job. He still limped from a bullet to the thigh the doctors decided not to remove, but he had proven himself to be a fair supervisor and administrator, respected by the other men.

Daniel dismounted and shook Jedediah's hand. "We don't see you here often, Mr. Whitcomb. You here about Jacob?"

Daniel nodded, keeping his focus on the men working. "Did Abraham tell you?"

"No, it wasn't him. Abe didn't show up today. Neville told me. Said he saw Abe bring the slave into town who killed the boy."

"There are no more slaves in this country, Jedediah, and there aren't any in Whitcomb Springs."

Jedediah removed his hat and wiped his sweaty brow with a dusty rag. "Sorry about that. Still getting used to the idea."

Daniel ignored the man's bigotry for the moment. "A snake bit Jacob. Cooper found the evidence on Jacob's arm. The conclusion is that Jacob fell from his horse, too sick to ride, and hit his head. Either way, he was unlikely to survive the bite."

"I was sorry to hear about Jacob. He was a good boy and hard worker. I'll make sure to end the speculating."

"Good." Daniel pulled himself easily into the saddle again and looked down at his foreman. "And release the men from work for the rest of the day. Tonight's celebration will still happen and they need help in town to set up. Anyone here now will receive a full day's wage."

"The men will appreciate it, sir."

"And Jedediah. Did Neville happen to say if he knew where Abe was going?"

Jedediah lifted his shoulders in a shrug, his face showing equal confusion. "He wasn't scheduled to work a shift today. I reckoned he was at home or in town."

Daniel thanked the man and rode back to town. Abe lived in one of the row houses built for the miners soon after Cooper discovered gold in their creek. One row of compact houses was nestled in a small clearing halfway between town and the mine. Most of the married men built small houses and cabins in town, or closer, for the safety and convenience of their wives and children. Daniel stopped there on his return trip to find Abe's place empty. He had not believed Abe would be at home, nor did he expect to find him anywhere else.

He rode the few miles home and noticed the scent of a fire already burning. The townspeople had accomplished a lot in the hour he'd been gone, and those already at the meadow would soon be joined by the men from the mine and timber camp. Each man worked only five days a week and never more hours than was healthy. Daniel decided to ask Cooper to have the foremen close down both sites tomorrow so the men could enjoy the remainder of the day without worrying about rising early. In their town, they couldn't get into much trouble. Maggie cut off drinks after three at the saloon, so if anyone planned to get drunk, it wouldn't be in town.

Meat would begin to roast over the flames and in another hour, the official festivities would begin. It had been Daniel's idea not to cancel, but now that the time of celebration neared, his apprehension rose to the surface. He backtracked and returned to the clinic, nodded to the two men still standing watch to make sure the body wasn't disturbed, and entered the building.

He crossed the wood floor and gently eased the canvas down and away from Jacob's head. "It was dumb luck that took you, but you deserved better. It was a hell of a way to go, Jacob. You made through the worst of the battles only to be felled by a damn snake. There are enough of us here, enough of us who made it out, to give you a proper send-off tomorrow." Daniel covered Jacob again, left the building, and rode home.

EVELYN SMOOTHED THE bodice of her dress. She had become used to foregoing a tight corset since leaving Pennsylvania, but tonight the dress would not close properly without tightened laces. Hany, thankfully, had been willing to assist. When she finished helping Evelyn into her dress, Hany left the room with a smile that left Evelyn wondering.

She turned to the right and left, examining her reflection from every angle. Her stomach and hips were still trim thanks to all the hard work in the gardens. She had grown stronger, but the change in her body was subtle. Evelyn smoothed her hands again over the delicate muslin and watched her eyes widen. Her waist had not thickened, but it did not take a lot for her body to fight against the seams of a carefully fitted gown. Her shock shifted to pleasure when she realized the meaning behind Hany's grin.

She and Daniel had spoken of starting a family, but that was before the war. When Evelyn didn't become pregnant, they wondered if it would ever happen for them. She knew with all her heart that Daniel would be as wonderful of a father as he had been a husband. "Is he ready?" She whispered the words aloud as she held her hands to her belly. "Am I ready?" Their time together since his return had been filled with days and nights relearning what they'd once known, and discovering new traits, likes, and dislikes they'd developed during their time apart. They were still the same people who imagined a house filled with children, but were they truly ready?

Evelyn fortified herself with a few deep breaths. Excitement and apprehension warred for first place in her thoughts, and it was a few more minutes before she guarded her emotions enough to descend the steps. Daniel waited at the bottom of the staircase, and nearby stood Gordon, Hany, and Grace. Evelyn had procured clothing for them from the general store that reasonably fit without alterations. It was Daniel's attire that caused her to falter and grip the bannister.

Daniel held out his hand and helped her down the final four steps. For her hearing only, he said, "You look magnificent."

"So do you." Since his return, Daniel's fine suits never left the armoire. The man before her looked more like the man she married. His eyes stood out as different. They'd seen much and revealed his suffering even when he tried to hide it. Tonight, his pain appeared to leave him alone, for in his eyes Evelyn saw only love.

"I cannot help but feel guilty with Jacob lying at the clinic while the rest of us celebrate."

"Do not worry about Jacob, my love. This is for him, too." Daniel did not elaborate and instead turned her attention to the others. "Gordon worries about his presence at the celebration tonight. I have assured him it is his choice, though perhaps some encouragement from you will help."

Evelyn walked two steps toward Gordon and his small family. "I have been false to all three of you, and to my husband. I have made assumptions about what your lives were like, about what you've endured. I told myself that I need only feel sympathy to understand, and yet the truth is, I know nothing. I cannot understand and I will not insult you by trying to imagine it. Whether it was chance or Fate that brought you here on this day, I will not speculate. This is a day for freedom and a time for healing. I know the establishment of our nation so long ago may not mean the same for you as it does for us—yet. However, I hope you will come to think of it as a day of hopeful beginnings."

Hany fingered the buttons on her new dress and looked shyly at Evelyn. "I don't reckon all folks will think like you."

"No, I suspect they won't, except here. In this town, every honorable person is welcome and has the chance to begin anew. You, my dear friends, are honorable people."

Hany tried to hide her sniffle. Young Grace did not fully grasp the meaning of what everyone said, but by the sweet smile and gentle tug on her mother's hand, Evelyn guessed that Grace understood happiness well enough.

THEY ARRIVED IN the meadow walking side by side with the Wells family. Silence descended on the crowd as all eyes, young and old, settled on their group. A few murmurs made the rounds until they were silenced by clapping. When Daniel looked from person to person, he realized they all watched the Wells family, and it was them they were honoring.

Not everyone joined in, and some dissention was to be expected, but Gordon, Hany, and Grace had been accepted. Daniel knew it was because they came as his and Evelyn's guests. He only cared that it was a start.

The townspeople had come together to enjoy good food, company, and a commemoration of independence. Tonight, there were no enemies, no sides, only friends and countrymen. The children sang "The Star-Spangled Banner" and "Amazing Grace," assisted by several adults. The first song roused the crowd, while the second cast a calm over everyone.

It was after the final lyrics to "Amazing Grace" ended that Daniel called on everyone to raise their glasses—with whatever filled them—to Jacob Smith, once a soldier and always a brother.

Toward the end of the evening, Daniel noticed his wife's distraction. "You're looking for someone?"

"Abigail. When Gordon returned, I went back to the school to speak with her. She wasn't there. I haven't seen her all afternoon."

"I suspect she's with Cooper. He had something he wanted to ask her."

Evelyn's arm was already linked with his and now her hand grasped his forearm. "Abigail has said nothing to me."

"I do not believe she knows."

"I had not realized. I mean, I knew it would happen. They love each other, and I already consider Cooper family, but it hasn't been long enough. They've only known—"

Daniel silenced her with a gentle kiss. "When there is never an assurance of tomorrow, it has been long enough."

"Cooper said nothing to me, either. Did he speak with you? There would not have been time to ask our father, and—"

Daniel figured what worked once would work again so he kissed her into silence. When their lips parted this time, Evelyn remained quiet, eliciting his grin. Daniel thought of his conversation with Cooper on the mountain only that morning. He had declared his love for Abigail, and for Daniel, that was enough. "Yes," he said. "You will be happy for them, won't you?"

"Of course!" Evelyn wrapped her arms around Daniel's neck, not caring who might see. "You're right, there is no need for them to wait a moment longer. She is my younger sister, though, so allow me a little anxiety on her behalf."

Daniel chuckled and noticed the objects of their conversation walking toward them. Abigail wore a beaming smile that brightened every inch of her face. Cooper was in much the same predicament. "Evie, love, turn around." She did, and the sisters embraced. Both allowed their tears of happiness to fall unbidden, and Evelyn was relentless until Abigail promised they would talk more in a few days.

Tomorrow they would hold Jacob's funeral.

Cooper pulled Daniel aside when Evelyn and Abigail were occupied congratulating the children on their beautiful songs. Cooper explained what he found in the search for Jacob's horse. "A farmer who lives a quarter mile west of town, Zeb Calhoun, saw a rider headed out pretty fast. He couldn't see much from where he stood in his field, but he thinks the horse was a buckskin, like Jacob's. I followed the tracks but that road is well traveled."

"Without a telegraph, we have no way to get word quickly to the nearest towns. A letter with a description, mailed to the neighboring areas, will have to suffice."

Cooper nodded. "Any word on when Abbott Jenkins will arrive?"

"Any day now. Although, you've made a pretty good stand-in sheriff." Daniel chuckled at Cooper's genuine groan.

"I'm not cut out to be accountable to people on a daily basis."

"What about Abigail?"

Cooper blinked. "Well, shoot."

Daniel and Cooper both shifted their gazes to Abigail when Daniel asked, "Having second thoughts?"

The smile on Cooper's face told Daniel everything he ever needed to believe his friend and sister-in-law were as true and real as he and Evelyn. Cooper walked away from Daniel, stopping only long enough to say, "It will please me to be accountable to Abigail every day for the rest of our lives together." He quickly qualified it with, "But only Abigail."

LATER THAT EVENING, when they all returned to the big house Daniel had built for Evelyn, they lay together in bed, limbs entwined. Daniel brought Evelyn even closer to his chest and inhaled the sweet fragrance clinging to her soft hair. "I have been thinking about the house across the road from us."

"The one James Bair built?"

Daniel nodded, thinking of his friend and one of the founders of Whitcomb Springs. He perished his first winter in Montana, and his house had remained empty since. "Do you think it would be a good place for a family?"

"Yes, I do. The Wells family could be very happy there. It's been kept in good repair and only requires a thorough cleaning. James only had a few pieces of furniture. We can bring in more."

"We could, though I think Gordon will want to build most of it himself."

"He's a craftsman?"

Daniel kissed the back of her head. Closer wasn't close enough for him. "He told me he built a few pieces for the family who owned him."

"Whitcomb Springs could use a man with his talents."

"Uh-huh." Daniel's hands moved from her hips, inching higher. "Evie. When were you going to tell me?"

He felt her stiffen for a second, then relax before she rolled onto her other side and faced him. "When I was certain. I only realized it today." She covered his hand when it moved to her flat belly. "How did you know?"

Daniel leaned in and brushed his lips over hers. Once. Twice. "I know your body better than you do. Some parts have . . ."

"Don't you say it, Daniel Whitcomb."

"In the presence of a lady, I wouldn't dare."

She laughed and swatted his shoulder. "Yes, you would dare."

Daniel sobered. He caressed Evelyn's cheek, her arm, and moved his fingers up and down the length of her, wherever he could reach. "I don't want you to have any regrets." He pressed a finger to mouth, preventing her from speaking. "Let me say this. I still have nightmares. Not as often, but they come when I least expect. The night I nearly choked you in my sleep was the worst night of my life."

"No." Evelyn rolled up and straddled him, forcing his arms

back. It was her way of gaining his full attention, and she had it. "That was not you. You woke up before any harm was done."

"I don't want to be a danger to you or our child."

"Do you really believe you will be?"

Daniel leaned up, pressing against Evelyn's grip on his arms until she released them. His hands found a comfortable place on the small of her back. "No. I am getting better. You've been more patient than I had a right to ask. I know there is still more for me to deal with, and one day—soon I hope—I will tell you what I haven't been able to share yet. One thing I know with absolute certainty is that I will never harm you again or our child, even during my worst nightmares. But it's important you know I will never—"

Evelyn's lips found his and swept him up in a kiss that evaporated all reason from his mind. Against his mouth, she murmured, "I never thought it. I had a moment today, wondering if we were ready, but I never once doubted your ability to be a father. You are the most honorable and loving man I have ever known. Our children will be blessed to have you."

Daniel shook his head and flipped his wife onto her back. "To have us."

THE FOLLOWING MORNING, Daniel donned his officer's uniform. Evelyn stared in awe at how marvelous he looked. She had cleaned and pressed the garments and found a place for them in the armoire, but he had not worn it for her before today.

She did not have to wonder why Daniel's countenance shined brighter today than other since his return. He had overcome the first of his internal demons, and the chains of fear and grim memories would continue to unravel, one day at a time. It would be a day of sadness and celebration as they lay Jacob Smith to rest in the town cemetery. And yet, Jacob would be remembered more for his passing because of the timing of his unplanned departure. Evelyn did not know how so much love could take place on a day of mourning, yet love filled her.

She and Abigail had a wedding to plan, and God willing, the child she carried would come safely into the world. Every dream and plan they had envisioned when they first stood atop the mountain and saw their untouched valley had been for this moment.

"Evelyn?"

She smiled at herself in the mirror as though she and her reflection shared a secret. "Coming, darling." Evelyn draped a paisley, silk shawl over her black dress and went to meet her husband so they could honor not only one soldier, but all who fell and all who returned.

WHISPER RIDGE

When he rescues a beautiful woman from the mountain lake, Clayton McArthur questions the secluded life he has chosen. Too many battles gave him enough scars and stories to last a lifetime, but reuniting with old friends and healing past wounds helps him to see a life beyond the memories of war. When a man from Gwen Armstrong's past arrives, and secrets are revealed, will Clayton return to his solitary life or trust in the gift only Gwen can give?

WHISPER RIDGE

LITTLE COULD COMPEL Clayton McArthur to lay down his pencil and turn his mind away from pleading eyes, bloody wounds, and cries in the darkest hours of night. Little else except a beautiful woman's sleek body gliding through unclouded water.

He willed his mind to turn away and leave her to the obvious enjoyment of her impromptu swim. Five minutes earlier, he had watched from his rocky perch as she set down a basket of wild berries, stripped down to her chemise and pantaloons, and dove into the crystal-clear mountain lake.

Mesmerized, he told himself a gentleman would at least make himself known. He could not leave his place on the cliff without walking the same trail he used to climb up. The trail curved around two sides of the lake, and his horse rested beyond there. Leaving without causing her some embarrassment was not within his power. The only sounds he heard beyond his thoughts were her splashes and the gurgling water that flowed alongside the trail to meet the lake.

Strands of amber hair escaped their confines when she floated above and skimmed below the water. He picked up his pencil again and applied it to paper before the image left his imaginings.

The details of her face remained a mystery, for he had only glimpsed fair skin before she sought the cool depths of the lake. The pencil fairly flew in Clayton's skilled hand, and her face emerged on paper. He gave her gray eyes without knowing for certain of their true color and scarlet lips because he wished them so. None of this came through in the sketch made with the charcoal tip, but in his mind, her vivid coloring was as clear as the sky above.

When she returned to the grassy bank and emerged from the water, Clayton forced his eyes away. Only when a soft cry traveled to where he knelt on the cliff did he look down again.

Clayton did not know how long he held his breath, or how his legs had carried him so swiftly down the steep trail to the water's edge, or even how he reached her before . . . he dared not think it. He lifted her from the lake's edge and carried her cocooned in his arms to where she left her clothes. She did not require his breath to rid her lungs of water, for she expelled what little she swallowed as soon as he laid her down on the grass.

He was more concerned with the watery blood seeping from the edge of her scalp. Ignoring her soft moans, he searched along her hairline and found the injury that caused her temporary unconsciousness. Blood on a rock nearby told him it was responsible. Clayton tore a strip from her dry petticoat and pressed the clean, white cloth to her head. He repeated the process with three more strips before the wound had stopped the worst of its bleeding.

Memories of other wounds—bloodier and debilitating— flitted through his mind. He cursed and fought them back, dragging his consciousness back to the woman in his arms. When had he lifted her again into his embrace? Clayton laid her back down and studied her face, not surprised at the accuracy of his sketch.

Her thickly lashed eyelids remained closed, even after repeated pleas for her to wake up. Five years had passed since he helped a woman into clothes—or out of them—but he knew what to do. Her legs went easily through the opening of what remained of her petticoat. The brown-and-white silk dress proved more difficult as he struggled to hold her up while slipping her arms through the sleeves. He thought little of the liberties he took as his fingers deftly buttoned the dress closed over her wet chemise.

He paused only once when his knuckle brushed against an something hard beneath the thin fabric. He checked her neck and felt the chain of a necklace. Ignoring it, he secured the rest of the buttons. Her corset remained on the ground. The stockings and leather boots proved easier.

Thankfully, she had not worn hoops on her outing.

Clayton mentally calculated the distance between them and his horse. Making sure she was secure where she lay, he ran to fetch Shiloh, the gray thoroughbred who had been with him since that fateful battle of the same name. When he returned to the woman's side, he found her in the same position and checked for a pulse and breath. Finding both, Clayton lifted her with all the care he would a child.

"Stay still for me, friend," he said to the horse. Shiloh did not even swish his tail when Clayton draped the woman over the saddle. He hesitated for a second before picking up her basket of berries and hooking the handle over the saddle horn before he stuffed her corset into his saddlebag. Careful to swing up behind the saddle, he lifted her into his arms and awkwardly moved forward until he was secure in the leather seat and she cradled on his lap. Her legs hung over one of his and his back and arm secured her against his chest.

He guided his horse onto the trail leading into the mountain valley where the quiet mining town of Whitcomb Springs flourished, thanks to Daniel and Evelyn Whitcomb. Clayton hoped their concern for one of their own outweighed their desire to run him out.

LATE AUGUST HEAT burned through Clayton's tan duster, and sweat dripped down his back, but he ignored the discomfort lest he shift and disturb the sleeping woman. Only one thing mattered to him as he peered down at her upturned face—that she recover quickly. His chest tightened when he realized the truth of his thoughts. He could not explain what had come over him, or why it mattered so much, but he needed her to live as much as he needed to breathe. His previous examination of the wound left him hopeful, but he'd witnessed numerous injuries a field doctor had deemed minor. How many soldiers died for lack of simple care? Too many. Another curse hovered on his lips, but Clayton held it.

Shouts drew him halfway to the present, and the soft form warm against his body brought him the rest of the way. A lithe and handsome woman walked down the steps of a porch that traveled the length of what appeared to be the largest house in the small town. When recognition and concern took over her gentle features, Clayton held his breath and then released it. Evelyn Whitcomb had recognized the woman in his arms, not him.

He, however, would know her anywhere, even after ten years. "Is there a doctor or nurse in town?"

Evelyn shook her head and reached out, only to grasp air as Clayton brought his horse to a stop. "We expected the new doctor to arrive last week, but he was delayed. What happened to Gwen?"

Gwen, meaning white or holy. Somehow, he knew the name suited her. "She fell and hit a rock. Where's the closest doctor?"

"Too far."

"Is the clinic stocked?"

Evelyn leveled her gaze at Clayton's shaded face. He saw no recognition in her eyes and thought it best. "Yes. It's down the street, the last building. I'll get my husband. He knows something about treating wounds."

"So do I." Clayton held Gwen closer and trusted Shiloh to carry them the rest of the way. Evelyn shouted for someone to get Daniel and rushed to catch up to them. By the time she entered the clinic, Clayton had laid Gwen out on the examination table. The spacious square room lacked the finer amenities of a city hospital or high-priced doctor's office, but a quick scan of the glass-fronted hutch told him it was indeed well-stocked.

"Watch her." Pleased to find a water pump and basin inside, he primed the pump a few times until he filled a bowl. He then primed it again and filled a second bowl, using this one to wash his hands. He found most of everything else he needed on the shelves and brought his bounty back to the table. "She's been unconscious the whole time, but I don't want her to wake up while I'm stitching her wound. Will you please hold her arms?"

Clayton heard a commotion outside and changed his mind. "Will you please close the door first and then hold her arms?"

Evelyn seemed content for the moment to follow his direction. When she returned to Gwen's side, she asked, "Where did you find her?"

"There's a long trail that goes up the mountain and a lake near the top with cliffs on two sides."

"Cooper's Lake." Evelyn wet a clean cloth and wiped away blood from Gwen's forehead when Clayton removed the temporary bandage. "She likes to swim up there. Most people don't bother when there are easier lakes and rivers to reach." Evelyn's voice choked a little. "But Gwen says that one is closer to heaven."

Comfort gripped his heart at the fanciful notion. Did he ever believe in something so hopeful? Darkening skies outside blocked some of his light, and Clayton wished he had thought to remove his hat before he started. He didn't want to stop and wash his hands again, so he left the hat on his head and tended to the wound. After checking the injury for any flecks of the stone that had cut her open, he cleaned it with water and a little alcohol and put in six neat stitches. "Would you mind asking someone out there to bring fresh honey?"

If Evelyn thought the request odd, she didn't say. Instead, she walked over to the shelves, found a jar tucked behind others, and handed it to him. "We've been treating minor wounds in here since the building went up, and most folks like what they're used to. That's fresh from two days ago when a miner cut his arm."

Clayton thanked her, removed the lid on the small honey jar, dabbed some on another clean cloth, and smoothed it over the wound. "The cut has stopped bleeding, and as long as she's careful, it should heal quickly."

"Why is she still asleep?"

He'd seen a lot less keep healthy men down for longer. Clayton plied off the lid of one more bottle, this one small, and hovered it beneath Gwen's nose. After four passes, she twitched her nose and her hand swung up to knock the offensive bottle of smelling salts from Clayton's hand. The tension left his shoulders and back, and a breath of relief escaped when he smiled.

"Gwen?"

Her eyes fluttered open. Gray. How did he know they would be gray?

"Can you hear me, Gwen?"

The slight nod was too much for her, so she followed it with a quick blink. "Who are you?"

"Gwen? It's Evelyn."

She shifted her eyes toward the soft voice. "Evelyn. I'm so sorry. I forgot the berries."

Clayton's smile remained when he leaned closer. "Your basket of wild berries is safe. Do you remember what happened?"

Gwen glanced left to right, one to the other, before she stared at Clayton. "I fell, but then everything else is blank." Her eyes squeezed closed.

"Don't force it. You slipped coming out of the water and hit your head on the sharp edge of a rock." Clayton sensed Evelyn's eyes boring into him and ignored it.

A smile flitted over Gwen's lips. "I didn't drown."

"No, you didn't drown."

"Who are you?"

A moment of reckoning came in many forms, and no matter how many times Clayton imagined this one coming about, he did not expect to be this unprepared. He was glad Daniel wasn't here, too, but then understood the awful power of fate when the clinic door opened and Daniel Whitcomb rushed in.

Clayton finally removed his hat. Without the protection of its shadow, or the distraction of Gwen's care, awareness swept over Evelyn's face. However, it was Daniel who spoke first when he closed the door and crossed the room.

"What are you doing here, McArthur?"

A PARCHED THROAT and piercing pain in her head kept Gwen from raising her head off the soft pillow. She opened her eyes, one at a time, and soaked in her surroundings.

Home. Her bedroom. The handmade quilt with a Celtic square pattern in green, gold, and white covered everything except her head. Even her arms rested beneath the blanket she had refused to leave behind when she ventured west. When she moved, confusion hit her senses first and shock quickly followed as her fingers brushed up against a bare thigh. Gwen trailed higher and relaxed when she discovered her nightgown merely bunched around her hips. A loud groan escaped when she tried to sit up.

"Careful not to move too fast."

The deep and familiar voice had her frantically searching the room. When her gaze landed on the doorway and the man standing beneath the threshold holding a tray, her heart decreased its rapid beats.

"Sorry to startle you. I had hoped to leave this for when you woke up." He jerked his head at the table next to the bed. "May I?"

Gwen raised the quilt back to her chin and nodded. "I don't recall that I asked your name before. I think . . . I heard Daniel call you McArthur."

Clayton's brief pause in lowering the tray onto the bed did not go unnoticed. She moved her legs lest she accidentally kick the tray from beneath the covers. "Is that your name?"

"Clayton McArthur."

"And you know Daniel and Evelyn?"

He nodded.

Gwen wanted to toss one of the soft biscuits at him. "I won't bother to inquire into how you know them since it seems to bother you." She looked from the tray up to him. "Thank you for this." She reached for the water first and drained half the glass to soothe her parched throat. "I am surprised Evelyn let you come here alone. After the tone Daniel used when he spoke to you, I . . . did I pass out again?"

"That's a lot of talking for someone with a sore head. Yes, you've been asleep for a few hours." A smile tugged at his mouth. "Your berries are no doubt baking in a pie as we speak." Clayton cleared his throat at the amusement from her face. "I'll leave you to eat and dress, or rest more if you need it."

"If I sleep again, will you be here when I awaken?" His lack of response gave her the answer she expected. "Is it because of the Whitcombs?" Surely no one could wish Daniel or Evelyn ill will. Gwen's time in their town was limited to the past two months, but it took less than a week to see how much they were both respected and liked.

On a heavy sigh, Clayton sat in the only chair in the room. "You may as well eat that while it's still warm."

"You're going to watch me eat?"

"I'm going to consider answering your last question while you eat."

He was obviously not used to teasing. Even as Gwen thought it, she scolded herself. How many men had she met these past months with the same hollowness in their eyes, a void so deep one did not have to look far before reaching their soul? Some men's depths were black as death, while others, like Clayton McArthur, held so much pain within. Their souls took the form of roiling storm clouds, ready to burst at any moment.

Gwen buttered one half of a biscuit and smoothed a layer of jam on top before holding it out for Clayton. His surprise evident, he accepted her offering, and she prepared the other half for herself. "I am not an invalid, but it was kind for Evelyn to send you with this. It still begs the question: Why did she allow you to come here alone?"

Clayton finished the biscuit before speaking. "That's another question, and I'm still deciding if I'll answer the first."

She swallowed her second bite, chewed, and then said, "I've asked a few. Will you respond to any of them?"

"I didn't give Evelyn much choice about letting me come here. It was difficult enough waiting in your sitting room while she helped you into your sleeping gown. If it soothes your nerves, she and Daniel are on the front porch, waiting for me. Much longer and they'll charge in to make sure you're all right."

"Mmm. I wonder." Gwen sat back against the pillow. "How do you know them?"

"From a long time ago."

"Daniel did not sound happy to see you."

"There's a lot of history between our families."

Gwen waited a few heartbeats for him to elaborate. "You are

not free with information." She waved away whatever he was about to say. "Never mind. I should not be so inquisitive. I'm told it is one of my greatest flaws."

"I would have said nosy."

Clayton spoke so softly, Gwen almost missed it. She grinned, unperturbed by his assessment. "My mother described it exactly the same way." Her grin faded, and she studied him with great interest, from eyes the color of a summer forest to the beard two shades darker than his sun-touched hair. Pain carved a path around his eyes. And she wanted desperately to know what had caused it. "Thank you for helping me."

His acknowledgment was a slight nod.

"What were you doing at the lake?"

"Deciding if I wanted to come into town."

"I rather forced your hand."

Clayton leaned forward and rested his forearms on his thighs. "You forced nothing. Given the circumstances, I can understand your curiosity—"

"Please, forgive the interruption." Gwen held up a hand for a few seconds before letting it fall back to her side on the quilt. "My curiosity is just that. I have no right to pry into your reasons for being here or into your history with the Whitcombs."

"I don't mind your curiosity, not really." He smiled and sat back. "I was writing and sketching on the cliff above the lake."

A rosy blush colored Gwen's fair skin. She did not ask how long he had watched her swim, and he did not offer a confession. His handling of her person left no question as to how much of her he had already seen. Gwen recalled wearing her dress, stockings, and shoes when she awakened on the padded table in the clinic. She only now remembered that she had been without a corset. Her fingers instinctively searched for the chain and ring she always wore, and found it pressed against her heart. "I'm grateful you were there."

His smile widened. "You're not going to ask what I was writing or sketching, or how I came to be in the spot at that time?"

Her mouth twitched as she held back a grin. "I deserved that." *Yes, I want to know everything,* she added silently. "It's Whisper Ridge."

"Pardon?"

"The cliff where you were. It's called Whisper Ridge." At his questioning look, she explained. "At dawn or dusk, it's believed you can hear singing so soft it sounds like a whisper. Fanciful."

"Sometimes people need fanciful. Have you ever heard the singing?"

She smiled. "Not yet. I'm also told at dawn and dusk is when a lot of animals are about, and I am not confident I could outrun a bear." Gwen's smile faded a little. "I would like you to answer one of my earlier questions, if you're amenable."

Clayton studied her for a full minute before responding. "Go ahead."

"Will you be here when I wake up again?"

The chair's legs scraped on the wood floor when Clayton stood. His long stride carried him slowly across the bedroom to the door, where he stopped, waited a few seconds, and then said over his shoulder, "I'll be here."

CLAYTON STEPPED ONTO the front porch and quietly closed the door behind him.

"I think she'll sleep a bit more."

Evelyn sat on one of the two wicker rockers while Daniel half-sat on the railing with his back against a column. Neither moved when Clayton spoke, and he took advantage of their continued attention.

"I imagined many situations in which we'd meet again, and present circumstances never fell on the list of possibilities." He shook his head when both would have spoken. "Explanations and apologies are owed, mostly by me. Too many years have passed, and I've grown comfortable with the 'what ifs,' but if you'll indulge me a few more hours, I'd appreciate it."

Clayton left them to think about what he'd said while he walked away from Gwen's house. toward the trees and away from his past. He found a winding trail sheltered by thick pine trees and continued, at first lost in thought, and then doing his best to push the last decade out of his mind.

Cannon bangs echoed in his ears before the expected crash and explosion. Smoke permeated the air, an effective shield to blind the enemy but also them. How many had died in the shadows of acrid smoke, when every man appeared the same until you were right upon them, either looking into their eyes or down their musket?

Wails vibrated between trees, once peaceful homes for wildlife, and over meadows and hills once abundant with fresh grass and wildflowers. He tried to bring back the beauty and serenity he remembered, but desecration kept pushing at the recesses of his consciousness.

A tall pine broke his fall forward, and only when he shook his head and returned to the present, did he realize he'd been running. He gave the protruding root a cursory glance and quietly thanked it for halting his maddening escape.

He closed his eyes and brought forth a more recent memory. High up a mountain trail, a crystal-clear lake reflected the colors and moods of the sky and shimmered beneath the sun. A woman, pure of heart, Evelyn had described her, glided through the water as though born to it. Clayton's breathing steadied breath by breath, heartbeat by heartbeat, until his legs could once more hold him tall and steady.

The return walk brought with it a breeze to dry his sweat and cool his skin. He took his time, wrote word after word, and stored the pages away until he would once more hold pencil and paper. By the time he emerged from the trees, the sun had moved high above, nestled among pillowy-white clouds.

Clayton knew their house since Evelyn had run from there upon first seeing Gwen in his arms. It suited them, he thought, more so than the imposing homes where they once lived in Pennsylvania. He'd been lucky to serve alongside two boyhood friends who still called their quiet northeastern valley home. They had shared with him news of family and mutual acquaintances but were careful not to speak of the Whitcombs. Later that evening, after they won the skirmish, Clayton sought them out to share a fire and swap more tales. Instead, he found them on the battlefield and buried them where they lay until he could return.

He would carry their scars and cries with him until he finished telling their stories. For now, Clayton pushed everything deep inside except what he needed to face two of his oldest friends.

THEY INVITED HIM into their home.

Evelyn offered Clayton a seat in her parlor, an unexpected gesture. He shouldn't have been surprised, though. Salt-of-the-earth folks, people would call them, and two of the kindest people he had ever met.

Regret had crawled deep into his gut ten years ago, and not even four devastating years of war had erased the festering guilt. Clayton knew he'd find more compassion from Evelyn, but it was Daniel's intense stare he met and held. The mirror image of his own horrors peered back at him.

Clayton and Daniel remained silent as Evelyn served tea. Another gesture of kindness he should have expected but did not consider himself lucky enough to have hoped for. Daniel's dusty clothes attested to work outdoors in a place removed from his lavish upbringing, and Clayton admired his old friend even more for it.

More guilt chafed Clayton for keeping Daniel from whatever else needed his attention. They'd waited for him, as he knew they would.

"She died five years ago," Daniel said.

A slow exhale of breath gave Clayton a few seconds to compose himself against those words. "I know." It was to Daniel he spoke—to Daniel, he ultimately owed an apology because he could not give one to Daniel's sister. "I learned of her passing last year from her husband."

"Her husband died last year as well."

"November 6."

Where Evelyn wore confusion clearly in her expression, Daniel nodded as though he understood. "You were with him."

Clayton drank from the delicate cup, downing half the spicy tea. For a few moments, he allowed himself to travel back to a time when he sat next to Leah Whitcomb, with Daniel and Evelyn on the opposite sofa, as he and Leah announced their engagement. He still tasted the same tea on his lips, a blend Leah had also favored.

He cleared his throat and set his cup back on the tray.

"You were a scout."

Clayton confirmed Daniel's statement with a nod. "Sharpshooter, but more often assigned to scout duty." He did not mention his time volunteering in a field hospital, and how he always prayed to die in battle rather than end up in one of the tents that constantly stank of death. "They assigned Jameson and me to scout nearby enemy camps before the next skirmish. We had learned only the day before that they took thousands of Union soldiers to Salisbury Prison. We planned to go there next, find a way in, and learn about their defenses. It wasn't our assignment, but they were our men, and that place . . . we promised each other that neither of us would end up in a place like that."

Caution tinged Evelyn's voice when she asked, "We never learned how Jameson died, only that it was on the battlefield. His mother wrote to us soon after she received the news."

A curse lay on the edge of Clayton's tongue, but for Evelyn's sake, he swallowed it. They should have been told everything, he thought. The men who gave their lives deserved better, as did their families. "We sought shelter in an abandoned barn during a storm and discovered a cache of weapons and luxury goods." He hated even recalling what had happened, and even more the retelling of it. "One smuggler returned, caught us unaware, and shot Jameson at the same time I pulled the trigger on my pistol."

Clayton eyed each of them. "You wondered for a minute if I

kept my promise to him." Evelyn's blush told she had thought it. At least she didn't ask if he would have shot Jameson to save him from prison.

Daniel remained standing for a long while as an uncomfortable tension filled the room. Voices from passersby on the street drifted in with a warm breeze through an open window. When at last he took a seat in the plush chair next to his wife, he stared squarely at Clayton. "Jameson was lucky to have you with him in those last days. He never came home to bury his wife, which by the look on your face he told you."

Clayton confirmed it as truth.

"Jameston loved Leah fiercely, even knowing the truth." Evelyn's words pierced through the apology Clayton had on his tongue.

Daniel drew Clayton's attention back. "Before she died, Leah confessed to our mother what she'd done. By then, you had already left Pennsylvania, and we came out here. Your lawyer refused to tell us where you'd gone."

Leah confessed? Clayton could not reason such a selfless act with the woman he had once admired, even believed he could have loved if given time. "I didn't want to be found. The business was under the capable supervision of the same men who oversaw matters for decades. They didn't need me underfoot. I came west to Colorado first, then returned when word of Fort Sumter reached me."

"Why didn't you tell us?" Evelyn asked.

Why? Clayton had asked himself that question countless times but held his council, even when his dearest friends believed he'd betrayed them.

Evelyn moved to sit beside Clayton and covered his large

hands with her delicate ones. "We all spoke such angry words the last time we sat together. You, though, I think, have suffered more than anyone else. Our inability to forgive sooner, and the blame everyone in our families cast on you . . ." A single tear dripped down Evelyn's soft cheek. "Can you ever forgive us?"

Clayton raised Evelyn's hands to his lips and pressed a kiss to each one. He did not trust himself to speak yet. He had loved Daniel and Evelyn more than any two people—more than the woman he was once going to marry—and losing them had been a dagger in his heart. With each battle and death the war forced upon them, the dagger sliced deeper, and he welcomed it. "You're all I have left."

Daniel and Clayton stood at the same time, as though driven by a force only those who had suffered could understand, and they embraced. In an unsteady voice filled with hope, Daniel said, "Welcome home, brother."

They spoke then of home, family, and their dreams of traveling west. He smiled at their joint recollection of how they felt when they first saw the mountain valley and knew they'd found their forever on Earth. He was surprised to learn that Evelyn's sister, Abigail, had followed in her footsteps and settled far from home. Married to Cooper McCord, Evelyn told him, the man responsible for showing them the valley. Clayton looked forward to seeing Abigail again and meeting the man who'd won her heart.

He heard Evelyn's great affection for Cooper when she spoke and noticed that Daniel heard it, too. Jealousy had never existed between them, but Daniel had missed out on four years with his wife, while life went on in Whitcomb Springs. Time, and Evelyn's love, could not erase Daniel's years at war, but together new memories had a chance to replace the old.

Clayton envied them desperately.

An hour later, he left the Whitcombs with each step lighter than the previous one. He stood on the wide dirt street and examined the town with an appraising eye. There wasn't much to it when compared with the Pennsylvania town where they'd all grown up. He liked it. A wildness still existed, threading its way into the makeup of the rustic village. Tidy buildings built of wood or stone offered little architectural wonders, but they stood solid, built to last by proud men and women who called this place home.

Wildflowers splashed across a nearby meadow, and profusions of color filled window boxes and small gardens. Townsfolk—mostly women—walked about, entering one building or exiting another. Most stopped to say hello to one another or make apologies for having to rush off. He'd asked enough questions in Butte before heading up the mountain road to know that the town survived on mining and timber. Clayton could imagine the effort required to haul both to the nearest railroad, but he could not imagine the train ever coming to this part of the country.

Where would he go from here? He planned to pass through on his way to explore more of the great Rocky Mountain west, perhaps venture into the Northwest Territories. As his legs carried him away from town, back toward the trail leading north to Cooper's Lake, Clayton considered the idea of staying still for a little while.

Restlessness had taken him from one town to the next since the war ended, and he'd help deliver his last comrade to his family in Kansas. From there, the wilder parts of the country beckoned him, for only the untamed landscape could understand the ghosts he ferried with him.

"Good thing you weren't a soldier."

Clayton waited for Gwen to come abreast of him.

"You heard me."

He smiled at the slight sound of dejection in her voice. "Were you trying to *not* be heard?"

"I wanted to speak with you but did not wish to disturb your peace. I was working through the dilemma."

Clayton inhaled the woodsy floral fragrance that belonged, he hoped, to her alone, the same scent that wafted from her hair when he had tended to her by the lake. They stood side by side, she half a foot shorter than him, and faced the mountains. Were it not for the occasional sound of life behind them, Clayton could imagine them completely alone, a state he preferred. Somehow, though, he did not mind Gwen's company. She drew his mind away from the harsher thoughts of yesterday.

"You haven't sent me away."

"You aren't disturbing me." A pair of eagles flew low, each one taking a turn at diving into the open meadow, in search of a meal. Seconds later, one captured its prey, and together they flew toward the trees. Her profile showed a faint discoloring peeked from beneath her hair. "How is your head?"

"Still attached and on the mend, for which I have you to thank."

Clayton did not offer a comment but merely gave a single nod. "You should rest more."

"I have rested enough, which is what I told Evelyn when she passed me a short while ago. I saw your horse in front of their house."

"What brought you here, Miss Armstrong?"

"Gwen."

He turned to face her fully. "Gwen. What brought you to Whitcomb Springs?"

MANY OTHERS had asked her the same question only to receive her practiced response. Gwen found she needed to tilt her head back a little, but not too much, to meet his inquiring gaze. Her palms no longer sweated when similar words were voiced by a curious townsperson, and after two months, most folks' interest had tapered off.

Because they didn't know the truth. Gwen digested the silent thought, and for the first time since she left home, she could not tell the same false story, though it wasn't so much false as incomplete. All of her family had died, and she had lost her fiancé. She left out the part that forced her to flee home.

"Redemption."

Clayton seemed to accept her answer and surprised her by not prodding for details. "I figure we're all seeking a bit of redemption these days."

Was he, she wondered, someone who would understand? Since her departure from home, she smiled and laughed and carried on as though her life began the moment she stepped onto the train in Atlanta. With each town Gwen journeyed through, she released a little piece of her past, until the last turn of a wagon's wheels dropped her off in Whitcomb Springs.

Every story she'd been told was true, and there in the mountain valley, surrounded by peaks rising above the clouds, she had found a home. Except it wasn't truly home because no one knew her. They only knew the person she wanted them to see.

"Do you believe an act, committed without malice—without corruption of one's soul—is sinful?"

Clayton blew out a low breath. "There's a question I figure most of us have asked ourselves a time or two."

Gwen blanched. "I'm sorry. I shouldn't have . . . that is . . . you were there, fighting, and I have no right to pose such a question."

In a gesture that surprised them both, Clayton grasped her hand when she walked away. "You mistook what I meant."

She returned to his side, but he did not let go of her.

"How did you know I fought in the war?"

It might have been an odd question considering the number of men who fought and died in battles across the western half of the vast land, but many more men never stepped foot on one of those battlefields. "You seem to carry too much pain, and there's enough of it around here to recognize the signs."

Clayton's fingers brushed across her sensitive skin when he finally released her. "I could say the same of you."

"Like recognizes like, my mother used to say." The war had touched most of the men and women in town in some way, and many of the ladies went on as widows, raising their children, hoping chance favored them with the courage to accept another husband. Gwen never had a chance to become a widow. "Perhaps—or not."

"I was sketching you from up on the cliff this morning."

The abrupt shift in their conversation forced Gwen to take a few seconds to rethink what she would say next. Trusting a person with the big confessions began with sharing smaller confidences. A blush warmed her skin when she recalled again the state of dress—or undress—when he had fetched her from the lake. "Before, you said you were writing *and* sketching."

His lips did not form a smile, but she saw a touch of mirth in the fine lines around his eyes and mouth. "So I did, and I was, but I had done little writing when I spotted you. I told myself to look away, and eventually, I did, but . . ."

"I have been swimming in that lake a dozen times and never slipped before. I don't remember everything, but now I recall the grass beneath my feet, slick from last evening's rain. Mud oozed through my toes, but it was a root that felled me."

"It's usually the small things that throw us off course."

Gwen heard her name in the near distance. She looked toward town and saw Tamsin waving at her. Gwen waved back and held up a finger, indicating she needed a minute. Tamsin smiled, nodded, and pointed at the general store.

"Are you expected somewhere?"

She nodded. "That's Tamsin Walker. She runs the newspaper, and I forgot I promised to help her select something at the store." Choosing fabric for a new dress was not something Gwen wanted to do. If she was honest with herself, she longed to be back up at the lake, gliding through the water, and spending the rest of the day in silence.

"Seems she could give you a reprieve, considering."

"We crossed paths before I came to find you. It's hard to cross the road, or even leave your house in the middle of the day, without someone stopping you to talk."

Clayton turned a half-circle and faced the entrance to town. "Whitcomb Springs warrants a newspaper?"

Gwen laughed before she could stop herself. "Not really.

Anything worth knowing makes the rounds in a few hours—a few minutes if it's urgent." She sobered a little. "Tamsin receives newspapers from all over the country. By the time they arrive, the news is obsolete, but she reads every one of them and puts highlights from articles into the town's weekly. She always includes a humorous tale from something that happened in town." Gwen cleared her throat. "Tamsin lost her husband at Sharpsburg. She was lucky to learn so soon after it happened, but there are still women here who do not know what happened to their husbands, fiancés, and brothers, and she does everything she can to help locate them."

"Did she help you?"

Clayton spoke in such a soft tone; the words seemed to caress her skin. "I already know what happened." A truth she never planned to share, and never wanted to—until now. She reminded herself this man was a stranger, albeit one who saved her life, but still an outsider who would likely be gone tomorrow. "I should go."

"Gwen?"

She peered at him over her shoulder, a brow raised in question.

"I'll still be here."

Her heart lurched when she sucked in a silent breath. She held onto the simple promise as she turned away and walked to the store.

THE CABIN OFFERED privacy yet sat nestled among trees close to town, another kindness from the Whitcombs. When Daniel showed up in the meadow not long after Gwen departed, it was with a key in hand and an offer of lodging.

"In case," Daniel said, "something keeps you from leaving too soon."

Clayton had long ago given up the comforts of his family's vast Pennsylvania horse farm, supported by their Philadelphia textile mills. The allowance once given to him by his father remained unchanged since he began traveling, and most of it went untouched. Knowing he could access whatever he needed at any time gave him the freedom to write his books and see the earnings were sent to the widows, whose husband's stories filled the pages. He had befriended many good men who sacrificed all, to their last breath, for the freedom of others and the love of home and country. They deserved more than a hole in the earth and a marker with only their name and date of death.

Each tale spoke of a man's courage, dreams, and bravery in battle, fictionalized for the sake of each man's family, but every word held a soldier's truth. His sixth work presently filled only two pages. Clayton owed it to his fallen friend to keep writing, to finish at a fevered pace as he'd written the others, and yet, this time, the words choked him. Jameson's family deserved the truth of a hero, son, brother, and husband.

He dropped his saddlebags on the table in the cozy kitchen. The only interior door opened into a single bedroom. A large stone fireplace covered half of one wall, and a hutch sat against another. The square wooden table filled the center of the room, and a cookstove in good repair stood to the right of the hearth. An outhouse stood a few dozen feet behind the cabin. Clayton was grateful it was still summer.

He lowered himself onto one chair by the table and wondered if the walls were closing in or if exhaustion only made it seem so.

The tintinnabulation of a loud bell clanged and banged through the air, drawing Clayton from the confines of the cabin. He was close enough to hear shouts mingle with each resounding echo from the bell, shouts that sounded too familiar. Fear and despair knew only one language.

Clayton heard a wagon's wheels speeding over the wide dirt road before he saw it. He rushed down the street from the cabin in time to witness a tall, black man pull the wagon to an impressive stop and shout for help. Clayton cut his surprise off and hurried to lend assistance. When he reached the wagon, a small crowd had gathered. He pushed through to the back and stopped. Two men, bloody and unmoving, lay on their backs.

Instinct took over, and he released the back latch, letting the wood slab fall against its hinges. Daniel stepped in beside him, and together they slid the first man out and carried him into the clinic. Daniel returned to the wagon to help carry in the second man. The man who drove the wagon closed the door and removed his hat.

"What happened, Gordon?" Daniel asked as he helped Clayton cut away the jacket and shirt from the first victim of whatever violence had taken place.

"I was tending the crops when I heard shots, so I ran toward 'em. Dem two was already down, and ain't no one else in sight. I hurried to fetch de wagon. They wasn't movin' the whole time, but I see they still breathed."

Clayton wiped some of the blood away and saw two bullet holes. He half-lifted the man to examine his back. "Both bullets went through. One in his shoulder, the other in his side. He's lost a lot of blood." Clayton moved to examine the second man who lay flat on the second table, his arms unwilling to stay up.

"This one took a bullet in his stomach." He asked Daniel, "Do you know either of them?"

Daniel shook his head. "They don't live around here."

"I's seen more tracks than what these two left," Gordon said.

"Could there be more?" Clayton made quick work of removing the coat and shirt.

"I's going back to look."

"No." Daniel placed a firm hand on Gordon's shoulder. "If there are more of them, it's best a few men go out there."

Everyone's focus shifted when the door opened. Evelyn and Gwen entered first, followed closely by Abigail. It momentarily struck Clayton how much Evelyn's younger sister had changed since he had seen her last.

He suspected the man brushing arms with Abigail was her husband, Cooper McCord, who sweaty, covered in dust, with a knife on his hip and a rifle in his hand, looked every inch a man of the mountains.

Cooper pivoted his wife and asked her to wait outside. He beseeched Evelyn to go with her. Gwen's chin tilted up in defiance. No one asked her to leave. She hurried to Clayton's side. "How can I help?"

Clayton pressed a thick white cloth into her palm and guided her hand to cover the worst of the two wounds. It had been ten months since he was in a field hospital, offering his hands where needed when the tents overflowed and there was nowhere else to put dying soldiers except to scatter them on litters outside surrounded by the heat, bugs, and stench of death.

"The bullet went through his arm, but this one got him in the gut, and it's still in there." He cursed the doctor that was late to arrive and glanced at Daniel. "The pain he'll suffer if we dig around for that bullet is going to be a lot worse than what he's feeling now, and it won't help him."

Cooper carried over alcohol and more cloths. Seconds later, the man took his last breath.

Without a word or thought, Clayton returned to the other man's side, grateful when Gwen joined him. "You're not squeamish?"

"No." She did not explain. "Will this one live?"

"Too soon to tell. He's lost blood, but I think the bullets missed his organs."

"Can you help him?"

"I'm not a doctor. We can clean and stitch the wounds, but the rest will be up to God." Clayton pointed to the man's head. "Will you turn his face toward me and check the back of his head? There's blood coming from somewhere."

Gwen moved to the other side of the table, but instead of doing as Clayton asked, her hands fisted over her heart.

"Gwen."

She stared at the face covered in a ragged beard.

"Gwen!"

Daniel stood beside her now, but it was to Clayton she spoke. "He's already dead."

Clayton checked for a pulse and breath. "No, he's not."

Her stare returned to the man's face. "He died six months ago."

Daniel caught Gwen before she tumbled to the ground.

SHADOWS PASSED OVER Gwen's line of vision every few seconds. As the blurred figure slowly came into focus, she noticed his eyes first. Warm, soulful eyes that had witnessed more than anyone should have to in a lifetime.

"I fainted." Gwen remembered the second before her vision went dark. "How long have I been out?"

"Twenty minutes."

Clayton helped her sit up and stuffed two of her pillows behind her for support. She was back in her house, in her bedroom, but this time fully clothed, and she and Clayton weren't alone. Evelyn set the washcloth she was holding on the edge of a porcelain bowl with water, which explained why Gwen's face felt cool.

"Twice in one day, Gwen." Evelyn shook her head and grasped her friend's hands. "Daniel said you fainted right in his arms. What happened?"

"You should have more care for yourself, Evelyn."

"I'm fine." She glanced at Clayton. "And so is the baby. It's you I'm worried about."

Still taken aback by the revelation of Evelyn's condition, he missed Gwen's question and asked her to repeat it.

"Is he alive?"

Clayton understood. "He hasn't woken yet, but he's still alive."

Gwen nodded slowly and looked out the window. Clouds had moved in to block the afternoon sun, and the air weighed heavy and damp. "Will he live?"

"If he survives the night, then he has a chance. He needs a doctor." Clayton lightly touched the sleeve of her blouse. "Who is he?"

Gwen shook her head and scooted to the edge of the bed. She found purchase on less-than-steady legs and walked from the room. Voices carried from the front porch through one of the open windows. Daniel and Cooper stood outside talking in tones too soft for her to make out the conversation. What had she been doing before the wagon arrived . . . oh, yes, Tamsin's fabric.

How is he alive? Did chance bring him here, or did he find out where'd she gone and follow? Dear God, how is he alive?

"Gwen?"

Clayton's voice broke through her thoughts. She did not have to turn around to know how close he was, or that Evelyn had not joined him. Seconds later, the front door opened and closed with a quiet click. The Whitcombs trusted him, so she could trust him, couldn't she? She had yet to tell her secret to Evelyn, and no other person could claim her friendship so much as the woman who helped her to start anew.

"He was my fiancé. I was supposed to become Mrs. Wilson Banks." Even now the idea of it made her stomach recoil.

"You thought he died in the war?"

She drew in a deep breath, counted a few beats, then exhaled enough of her fear to face Clayton. He stood half a dozen feet away, and his expression confirmed his curiosity. She shook her head and, no longer able to trust her strength, she lowered herself into a chair. Only that morning had she picked berries along the trail and enjoyed a swim in the peaceful waters of Cooper's Lake. How she wished she was still there, dipping her feet in the cool mountain water.

"I thought I had killed him."

Several seconds of silence drifted into minutes before Clayton spoke again. "Do you want to talk about it?"

Unable to contain tears she'd fought to hold back, Gwen gave in to the sobs as her shoulders shook. She could not say the precise moment when she realized how easily she fit within Clayton's embrace as her face pressed against his chest and her tears dampened his shirt.

The harder she cried, the tighter his arms encircled her in a protective shield she didn't know she needed until now. His voice penetrated the screams in her head, but her mind could not interpret his words. She heard the encouragement in his tone, and slammed her fist against his chest, once, twice, and a third time until his grip loosened. Clayton's arms remained around her until only even breaths escaped her lips. Even then, he waited for her to move away first.

When she pulled back and peered up at him, he brushed both thumbs across her cheeks to wipe away the remaining dampness. Tear stains and red-rimmed eyes remained, but with them, a clearer mind.

"What did he do to you?"

A hiccup escaped, and she covered her mouth against the next one. "I'm sorry. I shouldn't have . . ." She touched the spot on his shirt made wet from her tears. Gwen took another deep breath. "You don't ask if he deserved it?"

"I know he did, or you wouldn't have done it."

His unwavering faith in her, a stranger, amazed Gwen and gave her the courage to keep talking. "I didn't kill him, though. He's here. Why is he here?" She thought of the man she was once going to marry, and the man he'd become later. "The war changed him. When he came to see me—his first leave had been two years prior—madness had replaced the kindness. Wilson had changed so much in those years away."

"When was this?"

"January. I remember it was cold and dark the morning he showed up at my door. I turned him away that night, and three more times over the next few months."

"Did he desert?"

Gwen nodded. "He confessed that much the second time he came to the house. No one knew when the war would end, and I guess he'd had enough. I refused to go with him. When he came back the last time . . . he was so angry."

"What about your family?"

"Jimmy, he was my twin brother. I hadn't heard from him in months when Wilson showed up. Our father died at Bull Run, and Mother months later from fever. No one heard me scream when Wilson grabbed me—when he . . ." Gwen fought the memory back to the past. "The rifle Father taught us to shoot with hung on a rack by the back door, but I couldn't reach it fast enough. I grabbed the knife I was using to cut the venison meat one of my neighbors had brought over, and then it was quiet again."

"You've told no one this, have you?"

Gwen thought of the Whitcombs, of all the friends she had made in the two months since her arrival. With only a single carpetbag of belongings, and the money her parents had hidden beneath the floorboards in their bedroom, Gwen had arrived in Whitcomb Springs on hope and a prayer.

At some point, she had learned how to smile again, to laugh, and to enjoy the company of friends like before the war. "No, and they deserve to be told. I hoped to never leave here. I was careful when I left Georgia to take my time so no one could find me, even going to Texas before heading north. Evelyn and Daniel have been so good to me."

He tilted her chin up so their eyes met. "You don't think they'll understand? Had it been Evelyn, she would have done no different. You didn't kill him, Gwen, and if he dies now, it certainly won't be your fault."

"I need to know why he's here."

"Who knew you were coming west?"

"No one. Jimmy died at Petersburg."

Clayton brought her close to him again, and she willingly went. His energy soaked into Gwen, and she could not tell if it was energy born of eagerness, fearful frenzy, or because he didn't know what else to do at that moment. Her head tucked neatly beneath his chin, and she felt the vibrations when he spoke.

"It's your choice if you tell Daniel and Evelyn, but if Wilson wakes up, the truth will come out."

This time, when Gwen pulled back and stepped away so his hands dropped, she keenly felt the loss of his warmth.

Twenty minutes later, Gwen had told Daniel, Evelyn, and Cooper the abridged version of what she'd confessed to Clayton. She believed all three of them deserved the truth. She had learned early after her arrival that while every man and woman in town considered it their duty to keep their neighbors and livelihoods safe. If the townsfolk asked her to leave after what she'd kept from them, then . . . Gwen didn't want to consider it. She had nowhere else to go.

No, she clarified, there was nowhere else she *wanted* to go.

CLAYTON OPENED THE flap on his canvas satchel and withdrew the journal he used for drawing. The pages, ruffled by wind and specked with dust from having been dropped that morning on the mountain, opened to the sketch of Gwen. Now that he'd met her, held her, and wiped tears from her soft skin, Clayton noticed a few details missing from the likeness. He brushed away the dust and tucked the book back into his satchel. He then removed the last page he'd written in Jameson's story. He held the page in his hand as he lowered his lean form into the wicker rocker and stretched out his long legs. The sun had not returned yet after disappearing behind clouds tinged in gray. A cool breeze lifted dust and leaves and carried their spoils down the street.

In the two hours since Gwen had shared her secret, Clayton thought of little else except her. He gave her time and space, believing that's what he would want others to do for him, but after visiting the clinic to check on Wilson and walking from one end of the small town to the other, he found himself unable to remove her from his mind. When enough time passed, he returned to her tidy front porch and her wicker chair.

From where he sat, he could see Evelyn coming and going from her porch, her gaze always searching out Gwen's cottage for any sign of her friend. She stood there now, and when she saw Clayton, he swore the worry lines on Evelyn's face eased a fraction.

The cozy cabin waiting for him near the woods made him wonder how Gwen came by her cottage. Had someone else left it behind? He'd known plenty of folks who quickly discovered that an idealized life in the great western mountains was a lot different from actually living in them.

"How long have you been here?"

Clayton smiled and peered over his shoulder. Gwen leaned toward the open window and rested her arms on the sill. "Not long." He wanted to invite her to sit with him, but since it was her house, it wasn't his invitation to extend. "You look rested."

"Exhaustion has been my fate today." She glanced in the clinic's direction. "Has he awakened?"

"Not when I stopped in ten minutes ago. The man who found him—Gordon—is sitting with Wilson now. I'll relieve him soon." Clayton sat straight in the rocker and turned his torso to look at her better. "You don't have to see him again."

A soft sigh escaped her lips, but it was one of determination not defeat. "I left my home, my land, everything I knew and loved. This place has been a godsend, but a part of me still feels like I'm running away. I need to know what happened, and how he's here."

He waited several seconds, then asked, "Do you want to see him alone?"

Gwen shook her head. "I would like Daniel and Evelyn there . . . and you."

"If he wakes up, we'll all be there."

As though she no longer wished to speak of her former fiancé, Gwen pointed to the page he still held. "What is that?"

If she was back to being curious, then he supposed she must have her bearings again. He only wished she'd asked about something else. Clayton stared at the sheet of paper, filled from top to bottom with words that held great meaning but not enough feeling. He'd been unable to save Leah's husband, and how did one tell the story of Jameson's end without including that bit of truth. Leah was not alive to receive payment from the publication, and Daniel's family did not need the money, and yet . . . he owed it to Jameson—to Leah.

Clayton handed Gwen the sheet of paper with his neat script, then without a spoken word, he gathered his satchel and left.

THE CLINIC STILL smelled of death. Wilson's companion—whoever he was—had been moved and buried. It took Clayton and Daniel an hour, taking turns, to dig a hole six feet deep and large enough to fit the body. He offered Daniel no explanation as to why he wanted to help because the reason evaded him. Clayton crossed the room, pumped water into the sink basin, and cleaned what remained of the dark soil from the grave.

He thought of the man now buried, with no one to mourn his passing or visit his grave. The only scrap of paper found on the man had been a worn letter dated September 1863 and signed, "With all my love, Patricia." She'd addressed it as "Dearest" with no name. A simple cross marked the grave on the edge of the town's cemetery, with only the date scratched into the wood.

Clayton dried his hands while he leaned against the long table secured against the wall. Wilson lay in the same position since they finished stitching him up hours earlier. It took a great deal of willpower for Clayton to not shake the man awake and chase him as far away from Whitcomb Springs and Gwen as possible.

The door swung in and Daniel entered. "Expected I might find you here. I passed Gordon. Told him not to bother coming today."

"He has a family. No reason for him to deal with this." Clayton folded the damp cloth and set it aside.

"There's no reason for you to, either."

"Or you. Evelyn more or less told me she was expecting."

Daniel nodded and his genuine smile creased the edges of his eyes. "I learned a month ago, and I'm still getting used to it."

"Congratulations. I mean it. You both deserve every happiness."

The smile faded. "So do you."

Clayton leaned back on his arms and crossed one long leg over the other. "What did Leah tell you?"

"I wondered why you didn't ask before." Daniel kept the door slightly ajar to let air circulate through the space. "Not exactly the place for it." When Clayton continued to watch his friend, Daniel gave in. "She confessed it wasn't your child she lost."

"The truth then."

"You never defended yourself when she accused you or when others took her side."

Nor would he defend himself now. Clayton had turned Leah away when he found out about the child and questioned his choice every day since. Would he have taken her back had the child lived? He wondered often and always came to the same conclusion: If she had truly loved him as she claimed, she would not have given herself so freely to another man without regard to the consequences.

Daniel chose his next words carefully. "Leah was young. I won't make excuses for her because what she did, the lies she told to cover her own, was unforgivable."

Clayton crossed his arms and gave himself a few seconds to enjoy the winsome face of a young woman he once fancied. The image flitted as quickly as it came. "And the beating she said I gave her?"

"I never believed her about that, Clay. Neither did Evelyn. Our mother, however, couldn't be convinced otherwise."

"Who did it?" Clayton ground out the words.

Daniel's brow raised in surprise. "You don't know?"

"As far as Leah was concerned, I got her with child and blackened her eye."

A curse escaped Daniel's lips. "He worked in the stables. It seemed he thought fathering her child gave him a way into the family. We dismissed him the day we found out." Daniel's sigh was of a man filled with too much regret. "I loved Leah, and when she finally told everyone the truth, I believed—hoped— that she would find a way to make amends."

"Jameson said much the same."

"You talked to him about it?"

Clayton shook his head. "He did the talking, hoping I would understand that she had changed." He pushed away from the table and walked a few feet to stand over Wilson. "We both know how much war can change a person."

Understanding the direction of his thoughts, Daniel said, "Gwen doesn't have to see him."

"She will. Her choice. He might have gone mad, or he might have been a coward. It doesn't matter." Clayton lifted only his eyes to look at his friend. "He won't hurt her again."

"Agreed. We take care of our own here, Clay."

Clayton smiled at Daniel's use of the shortened version of his name for the second time. It took him back again to their youth and realized that no matter how many decades passed, the bond of friendship had been twisted and stretched yet never broke.

"What are your plans?"

I don't know, he said to himself. The page from Jameson's story, still with Gwen, deserved to be rewritten, and then the story finished. Clayton realized then what had been missing all along. It wasn't just Jameson's story, but Leah's as well, and all the other men who died and the women who never had a chance to say goodbye. By blocking Leah from his mind, he had blocked everyone else who mattered.

"Clay?"

He returned his thoughts to the present and studied Wilson once more. It was his story, too. "Fine. I'm fine."

A knock sounded on the ajar door, and a wiry man with a clean-shaven jaw stepped inside. "I've come to relieve Gordon."

Daniel waved him over. "Good timing. Gordon has left for the day. Buck Walker, this is Clayton McArthur."

Buck held out a hand to shake Clayton's. "Heard about you from my missus. Any friend of Daniel's is a friend to us all."

Clayton wondered who Mrs. Walker was and how she knew him already. Then he remembered Gwen's fabric outing with Tamsin Walker. "Thank you for the kind welcome." He studied Wilson's prone body and expressionless face once more before giving his attention back to Daniel. "There's something I have to do."

He did not return to Gwen's cottage for the sheet of paper or to ask her opinion. He would but not yet. Clayton's casual stride to the cabin he temporarily called home belied the rapid beat of his heart and tumultuous workings of his mind as he wrote out each word. First in his thoughts, and then when he reached the cabin and took out fresh paper and two pencils. He wished a quicker method of putting down words existed, but until then, Clayton would have to slow his ideas to match the pace of his writing.

For hours, he hunched over the small wooden table and abandoned his task only once to search for a lamp and by luck, found a single brick of matches. He broke one off and struck it on the stove, turning his head away from the pungent smell and initial flare. The lamp provided enough light for him to continue working. When darkness fully enveloped the world outside the cabin and the air grew as cold as some of the nights he had spent huddled in the rain, praying for the end of the war, he welcomed the memories.

It was the unmistakable tapping of a woodpecker that roused Clayton from sleep. His face winced and his body bunched when he lifted his head off the table too quickly. The initial pain shot through his neck and shoulders before finding a path down his back. Sunlight, the kind of soft, filtered light unique to early morning, filled the cabin. The lamp's wick had burned out during the night. When Clayton peered down at the stack of paper covered in thousands of words, pain and exhaustion fled.

He had a long way to go, but it was a solid beginning. His body fought against the stretch when Clayton first stood, then eased into it as his muscles loosened. He rubbed a hand over his jaw and decided he needed a bath before going to see Gwen.

Clayton reluctantly made use of the outdoor privy, then followed the sound of flowing water to its source. A creek carved a path through the forest and burbled as it traveled over and around rocks. Not as good as a bath but sufficient until he could find a place to soak in a tub filled with hot water. He stripped down to his pants, leaned over the creek, and splashed icy water over his arms, chest, and face. It wasn't the first time he'd bathed in water cold enough to raise bumps on his skin, and it had the added benefit of bringing him fully awake.

Twenty minutes later, with a rumbling stomach and desire for clean clothes, Clayton headed for Daniel's barn where Shiloh was stabled. He found the horse content and nickering with the two others in adjacent stalls. His saddlebags hung over a nearby rail, and from them he withdrew a clean shirt and changed. The rest, including laundry, could wait. For the first time since he struck out west again after the war ended, he wished for a permanent roof over his head and all the conveniences that provided.

The dirty shirt slipped from Clayton's grasp as a coldness swept through him—a chill like the sensation before a battle or when he felt someone watching him from afar while scouting. Awareness took him from the barn into the morning light where near-silence greeted him. A dense layer of mist had descended upon the mountain valley, and his eyes adjusted to make out shapes of structures.

A horse's hooves clopped on the road, and a wagon's wheels turned at a slow pace. Beyond those sounds, he heard nothing to indicate others were awake at the early hour. A day in town and he had already memorized the most important places. His legs now carried him through the mist, down the center of the road, toward Gwen's small wood-sided cottage. Her front gate lay open, and he could not recall if it was open the day before.

The quietude should have calmed him. Instead, he walked with cautious steps to the narrow porch. Clayton held his breath for a few seconds then released on a slow exhale. He repeated the routine to keep his heartbeat low, just like he learned to do as a sharpshooter. Calm, control, and confidence—those three words echoed in his mind. His booted foot contacted the first step up to the porch. A slight creak stopped him from putting any more weight on it.

Footsteps close drew his attention, and Daniel appeared at the gate. He came close enough so Clayton could speak in a whisper. "What are you doing here?"

"I'd ask the same of you, but I saw you when I was walking by. I checked on Wilson at the clinic."

"He's still there?"

Daniel nodded. "Not breathing well, either. The reverend is with him now. It's unlikely he'll make it to sunset."

Clayton absorbed the news and turned back to the house. "Does this cottage have a back door?"

"Yes." Daniel needed no prodding to quietly leave and circle to the back of the house. Clayton didn't wait. He ascended the three steps to the porch. Through an ajar window, he heard muffled voices, and what sounded like a soft whimper. Footsteps—one heavy, one light—followed until he saw Gwen walking backward. A man held a pistol pointed to her chest, and for every step he took toward her, she stepped back, staying just out of his reach.

They disappeared from view, but Clayton heard the man's words clearly. "Where is it?"

"I don't have what you want."

Amazed at Gwen's calm, Clayton reached for the doorknob and held his hand steady, hoping for a distraction.

"He said you have it!"

"Wilson was wrong."

Clayton heard them move toward the kitchen. He turned the knob a half-inch at a time, knowing he would have to be the distraction, and trusting Daniel to be there when needed.

"You'll hand it over, lady."

The man's words came harsher now. He was fast losing patience. Clayton eased open the door and stepped inside, his footfalls heavy on the wood floor and rug. Three seconds later, the man aimed the pistol at Clayton's chest, then his head, unable to decide the more prudent target.

"Even with the gun, your outlook is not promising. You can shoot me, but I promise you won't leave this house alive."

The man bit the inside of his cheek, and with wide eyes, stepped one foot closer to Clayton. "I kill her and you, then I'll get to wherever I want."

"What do you want?" Clayton gave the man a chance to feel in control.

"She knows."

He had avoided looking at Gwen before, but Clayton allowed himself a glance now. With a straight back and eyes focused on the gun pointed at Clayton's chest, Gwen appeared calm on the outside. With the slight quiver of her lips, and how she fisted the cloth of her skirt tightly within her grasp, Clayton knew she was close to an edge but would remain strong.

"Obviously, she doesn't. If you tell me—"

The man leaned forward, his feet still planted in place. "You her man? You know where she keeps her secrets?" A sick grin revealed lightly yellowed teeth except one in front darkened from decay.

Secrets? Clayton replayed the few conversations he'd had with Gwen, and only one thing came to mind. "You mean the money?"

Gwen gasped. He didn't acknowledge it.

"Yeah, the money." Ignoring Gwen now in favor of Clayton, the man waved a hand around the room. "You know where it is."

Clayton studied the man, uncertain what it was exactly that didn't add up. "I do. Gone."

The man's grin faltered. "Can't be."

"Three hundred dollars doesn't—"

"Wait. What now? Three hundred you say? No, I want the diamond."

"Someone has misinformed you." He closed the distance by another foot. What did he really want? "Now that you know there's nothing here, you can leave this house peacefully or you can leave it dead. It doesn't make a difference to me which you choose."

Clayton knew the moment Gwen saw Daniel and prayed for her to stay quiet. What he didn't expect was for her to draw fire. She advanced, forcing the man to lose his focus on Clayton. The pistol pointed first at her, then back at Clayton, before settling on Gwen when she ran into the next room.

The struggle lasted only twenty seconds but seemed to go for much longer. Clayton counted each second in time with his heartbeats. He couldn't recall how he came to hold the pistol in his own hands or at what point Daniel came from behind and snaked an arm around the assailant's neck. Clayton's right fist connected with the flailing man's jaw and knocked him unconscious.

"Gwen!" Clayton found her before she returned. She clutched her hand to her chest, and a long, gold chain dangled from between her fingers.

"I'm so sorry." Her hand loosened, and she held her palm out. "I couldn't give it to him." Attached to the gold chain, a ring of gold with two crossed stones—one diamond, one sapphire— rested in the center of her palm.

Clayton knew something of fine jewelry, for he'd seen his mother and others in their society circles back home wear enough jewels to recognize quality when he saw it. "Where did you get this?"

"It belonged to my mother. It was all her parents gave her when she left home to marry my father." Gwen dangled the ring by its chain. "It was meant to be my dowry."

"So Wilson knew of it."

She nodded. "I never imagined him alive, and even alive, why come so far for a little money and—"

"Gwen. Do you not know its value?"

Her eyes, filled with confusion, raised to meet his.

"More than Wilson, or his friend in there, would have seen in a lifetime."

She smoothed a finger over the stones. "My mother never told me. I wear it every day. Always." She glanced up at him. "Why would he come all this way, though, even if it is worth what you say?"

Clayton raised her chin with the edge of his fingers. "I suspect he wanted more than the ring."

"You're wrong. I'm nothing to him."

"Revenge can make even a sane man crazy."

"Are you all right, Gwen?" Daniel asked.

Gwen suppressed a shudder and peered around Clayton. The tension lines around her eyes and mouth smoothed a little into a half-smile. "I am now. Thank you, Daniel. Both of you. How did you know something was wrong?"

Daniel shook his head. "I didn't. When you're done, Clay, I'll need help to get this one over to the jail. Did he tell you his name, Gwen?"

"No. He only mentioned Wilson's name."

Daniel nodded and left them alone once more.

Gwen asked her question again, this time only of Clayton. "How did you know?"

Clayton brushed the tips of his fingers over the sides of her soft face. "A feeling. I can't explain it any better than that, at least not yet."

Her hand covered his, and together they slid down and rested over her heart. "Thank you for whatever brought you here to us."

Six months later . . .

THE BASKET GWEN carried bumped lightly against her leg as she walked up the mountain trail to Cooper's Lake. She'd forgotten her hat again. Clayton studied her from atop the ridge, where he'd been since the sun crested the mountain peaks. He waited and listened for the whispers Gwen spoke of, but it wasn't a soft song he heard in the air.

From the twittering songbirds came voices of comrades while they sat around a campfire and talked of boyish adventures and the families left behind. With the almost silent hopping of a mountain cottontail, came the waiting, wondering, and gratitude for his brothers-in-arms. Arising from the rustling leaves, he heard the sounds of war and home, of life, death, and rebirth. Each one whispered a memory he no longer tried to shut out.

Gwen reached the edge of the water and knelt in a patch of grass. She brought him back from the edge of darkness with her courage and hope. Clayton would never forget a single moment, but he'd finally found the words to do them justice.

Smiling, he stood, brushed off his pants, and walked the

narrow trail down to the lake.

"I thought I'd find you up here." Gwen patted the space next to her. Clayton needed no further encouragement, and he lowered himself to the grass before lifting the edge of the cloth covering whatever she held in the basket.

She swat his hand away. "Not yet."

His boyish grin remained when he leaned over to brush a kiss over her soft lips. "Payment enough?"

Her laughter cut through the quiet morning. "You're incorrigible."

No, Clayton thought, not incorrigible. Happy. Somehow, after more than a decade of loss, pain, and war, he learned how to be happy again. "Does that mean I get to see what's in the basket?"

She held up the edge of the cloth farthest from him and withdrew a muffin before covering the basket once more. Gwen handed him the offering with a smile. "Satisfied?"

Clayton almost choked on the first bite. "Hardly, but it's a start."

Gwen leaned over to scoop up some water and flicked it in his direction. He yanked her across his lap, dropping the muffin in favor of her warm body pressed to his.

"What are you—"

He kissed her soundly, transferring droplets of water from his skin to her. With aplomb, he set her back on the grass and picked up the crushed muffin. "No sense in wasting this."

The gold chain holding her mother's ring slipped from beneath her blouse. Clayton palmed it briefly before tucking it away. She wore it always still, regardless of its cost, but the ring far more precious to him was the one she wore on her finger.

The next time she reached beneath the striped cloth, her teasing had subsided. Her gray eyes glistened with tears but not of sadness. What she presented to him next was wrapped in brown paper and twine, and Clayton didn't need to ask what lay within.

"The supply wagon came through this morning. This was in it."

Reverently, he pulled on one edge of the twine, then the other until it fell to his lap. The paper followed to reveal a hardbound volume with one-hundred twenty pages of carefully typed words. He lightly touched the gold lettering and read aloud, "*Whispers of Truth: Tales of Courage and Honor.*" On the first page, instead of his name, it read, *Written by a soldier for his brothers-in-arms.*

Gwen picked up a letter that rested in the folds of the paper. "You missed this."

Clayton passed her the book and unfolded the letter. He read it once to himself, then to Gwen.

Dear Mr. McArthur,

We are pleased to inform you that the copy you hold is from the second print run of your book. As requested, we will pay all of your earnings in equal part to your list of names. Should you write another book to follow, it would be our great pleasure to publish it as well.

Sincerely,
P. Wylan
Wylan-Morgan Publishing House

"Will there be another?"

He tucked the letter away in the book. "No. I wrote what needed to be said for them and their families, and now . . ." Clayton pressed a hand gently to the soft swell of her stomach. "Now, it's time to look forward." He stood and then helped Gwen to her feet. Hand-in-hand, they walked along the trail, and when they reached the end of the lake, Clayton pulled her into his arms. With her back against his chest, he wrapped her in his embrace.

"I wonder if Daniel and Evelyn realized what they were building when they first came here."

Clayton kissed her neck, then rested his face against her hair. "They knew."

Daniel and Evelyn's vision for Whitcomb Springs started with an adventure to explore and live in the untamed West, but it was from faith and hard work, bound by their love, that arose a place of solace and new beginnings. Clayton held his wife closer, always mindful of her gift to him—her unconditional love. Their story was not the first, nor would it be the last. So long as the mountain valley welcomed those who had lost and loved, there would be a place for those who wished to hope and dream.

Thank you for reading
Hopes & Dreams in Whitcomb Springs!

View more about the series, including more stories from other authors, at www.mkmcclintock.com/whitcomb-springs-series.

If you enjoyed this story, please consider sharing your thoughts with fellow readers by leaving an online review.

Don't miss out on future books!
www.mkmcclintock.com/subscribe

Thank you for joining our adventures in Whitcomb Springs!

CROOKED CREEK SERIES

Four courageous women, an untamed land, and the daring to embark on an unforgettable adventure.

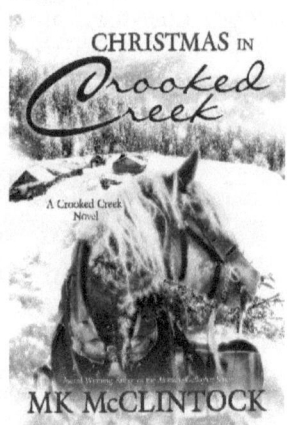

If you love stories of bravery and courage with unforgettable women and the men they love, you'll enjoy *The Women of Crooked Creek* and *Christmas in Crooked Creek*.

Available in e-book, paperback, and large print.

THE MONTANA GALLAGHERS

Three siblings. One legacy.
An unforgettable western romantic adventure series.

Set in 1880s Briarwood, Montana Territory, The Montana Gallagher series is about a frontier family's legacy, healing old wounds, and fighting for the land they love. Joined by spouses, extended family, friends, and townspeople, the Gallaghers strive to fulfill the legacy their parents began and protect the next generation's birthright.

Available in e-book, paperback, and large print.

McKenzie Sisters Series

Cassandra and Rose McKenzie are no ordinary sisters. One is scientifically inclined, lives in Denver, and rides a bicycle like her life—or a case—depends on it. The other rides trains, wields a blade, and keeps her identity as a Pinkerton "under wraps."

Immerse yourself in the delightfully entertaining McKenzie Sisters Mystery series set in Colorado at the turn of the twentieth-century.

Available in e-book, paperback, and large print.

BRITISH AGENT SERIES

Three men willing to risk life and duty for honor. Three women willing to risk everything for love and family.

From England, Scotland, and Ireland, the agents and the women they love embark on exciting adventures to save those closest to them.

"Ms. McClintock succeeds in masterfully weaving both genres meticulously together until mystery lovers are sold on romance and romance lovers love the mystery!" ~*InD'Tale Magazine*

Available in e-book, paperback, and large print.

A HOME FOR CHRISTMAS

Enjoy *A Home for Christmas*, a collection of heartwarming Christmas stories for any time of the year. Set in Montana, Wyoming, and Colorado in the 1800s.

THE AUTHOR

MK McClintock is an award-winning author who writes historical romantic fiction about chivalrous men and strong women who appreciate chivalry. Her stories of romance, mystery, and adventure sweep across the American West to the Victorian British Isles with places and times between and beyond. MK enjoys a quiet life in the northern Rocky Mountains.

Visit her online at **mkmcclintock.com**.